THE SWORD IN THE STONE

THE LEGEND OF KING ARTHUR

Adapted by Peter Oliver

Illustrated by Rex Archer and Lynne Willey

BRIMAX · NEWMARKET · ENGLAND

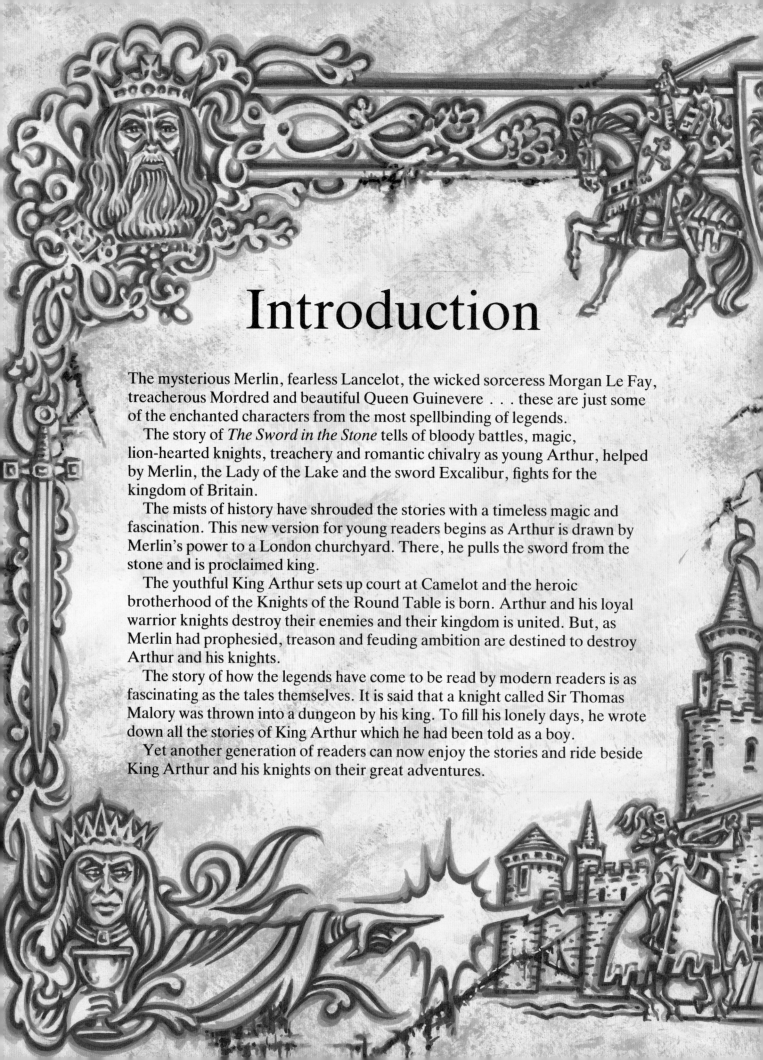

Introduction

The mysterious Merlin, fearless Lancelot, the wicked sorceress Morgan Le Fay, treacherous Mordred and beautiful Queen Guinevere . . . these are just some of the enchanted characters from the most spellbinding of legends.

The story of *The Sword in the Stone* tells of bloody battles, magic, lion-hearted knights, treachery and romantic chivalry as young Arthur, helped by Merlin, the Lady of the Lake and the sword Excalibur, fights for the kingdom of Britain.

The mists of history have shrouded the stories with a timeless magic and fascination. This new version for young readers begins as Arthur is drawn by Merlin's power to a London churchyard. There, he pulls the sword from the stone and is proclaimed king.

The youthful King Arthur sets up court at Camelot and the heroic brotherhood of the Knights of the Round Table is born. Arthur and his loyal warrior knights destroy their enemies and their kingdom is united. But, as Merlin had prophesied, treason and feuding ambition are destined to destroy Arthur and his knights.

The story of how the legends have come to be read by modern readers is as fascinating as the tales themselves. It is said that a knight called Sir Thomas Malory was thrown into a dungeon by his king. To fill his lonely days, he wrote down all the stories of King Arthur which he had been told as a boy.

Yet another generation of readers can now enjoy the stories and ride beside King Arthur and his knights on their great adventures.

Contents

The Sword in the Stone

Uther Pendragon, King of all England, lay dying as the first snow of winter settled on the castle battlements at Camelot. The knights and nobles of England, kings from Scotland, Wales and Ireland and powerful warlords from France surrounded his death-bed. In one corner of the room sat Uther's queen, Igraine, and their daughters, Margawse, the eldest, and young Morgan Le Fay. Closest to the bed stood Uther's most trusted men, the proud knights Sir Ulfius, Sir Brastias and Sir Baudwin.

The king was speaking in a dying whisper: 'Who will rule my kingdom when I'm gone?'

Most of the powerful men in the room were asking themselves the same question. 'Uther has no son,' they thought. 'Who will be king when he dies?' Some were already plotting to steal the kingdom for themselves.

8

Suddenly the great oak door in the room swung open. Everyone's eyes turned. At first they could see no one. It was as if the door had opened by itself. Then a figure appeared, moving slowly out of the shadows of the doorway. It was a wizened old man. Snow covered his hair and long icicles hung from a wild, grey beard.

'Stand aside,' said the ghostly apparition. 'I must speak with the king.'

'Get out!' said one knight. 'The king will not speak with the likes of you.'

The chilly visitor was unknown to most in the room. Yet, three people knew him well. He was no stranger to Ulfius, Brastias and Baudwin.

'You had better let him pass,' warned Sir Ulfius.

The knight still stood in his way. 'The king will not be bothered by this vagrant.'

The old man didn't seem concerned. 'No matter,' he said. With that, he faded into the shadows and vanished completely.

'A ghost!' shrieked King Anguish of Ireland.

'A phantom!' cried King Lot of Scotland.

'I am no ghost, even if some do call me a child of the Devil,' cried the old man. 'I am Merlin.'

9

They turned around and saw, to their astonishment, that the figure had reappeared right beside King Uther's bed. Some of the knights reached for their swords, but Merlin simply raised his hand and froze the great iron blades in their scabbards. Pull as hard as they might, not one could remove his sword.

'Now stand back,' said Merlin. 'I have private words to say to King Uther.'

The mightiest warriors in the land nervously shuffled back a few steps as Merlin's crooked body leaned over the king. He whispered a few words in the dying man's ear. Merlin's task done, he moved away from the bed. Knights and nobles alike moved aside as Merlin passed between them and disappeared through the doorway. A puddle of melted snow beside Uther's bed was all that was left to show that someone had been there.

'I have heard the sweetest words,' said Uther, gasping for breath. 'Merlin has made me happy in death.'

And with that, Uther, King of all England, died.

All the knights, nobles and kings returned to their castles; some to await news of who would be king after Uther, others to plan their attack on the kingdom. They gathered armies and ordered blacksmiths to their anvils to hammer iron into swords. They were not to know that Merlin was already at work, making a sword on his own anvil.

The armies marched out to battle for the crown. From the North, from the East, the South and the West, they came. Soon the wintry snows covering England's green land were stained with blood. Death stalked the countryside. Battles were won and lost and many thousands died. But no one man could gain control of King Uther's Christian kingdom.

Worse was to come as heathen invaders from across the sea reached England's shores. The bloodiest of warriors, they burned down villages and hamlets, killed all the men and took the women and their daughters for slaves.

'Who will save us now?' wailed sad voices from across the land as England bled.

There was one person who had the answer and he knew the time had come. Merlin flew by night to visit all the most powerful nobles. He sneaked into their dreams with a message.

'Make your way to London on Christmas morning,' he whispered, 'and a new king will be chosen from among you. Merlin has spoken.'

As Christmas approached, the roads to London thundered to the sound of horses carrying the men who would be king. They gathered on Christmas morning at the largest church in the city, and talked about their strange dreams. Everyone had heard Merlin's voice telling them to come to London. 'But how will the new king be chosen?' they puzzled. They were still confused when they went into the church to attend the morning service. Afterwards they walked out into the churchyard.

'Look!' cried Sir Ulfius, King Uther's loyal knight. 'What's that?'

In a corner of the churchyard, protected from the snow by a spreading yew tree, a huge marble stone had appeared. A great anvil of steel was set into it. And, stuck firmly in the anvil, was a gleaming sword.

Sir Ulfius, Sir Baudwin and Sir Brastias hurried across. 'What sorcery is this?' said Sir Brastias. 'This was not here when we went into the church.' Just then Sir Ulfius noticed some words which had been inscribed in gold along the blade of the sword. The three men read them in wonder.

"THE MAN WHO PULLS THIS SWORD FROM THE ANVIL IS THE TRUE-BORN KING OF ENGLAND".

'What does it mean?' asked Sir Brastias.

'There's only one way to find out,' said one boastful knight. 'I will pull out this sword and then I shall be the rightful king.'

The knight stepped forward and grasped the huge sword by the hilt. He pulled with all his strength. It would not move. He tried again and eventually tumbled backwards with his effort. But the sword remained in the anvil.

Another knight leapt forward anxious to prove that he was the chosen king. But the result was the same. He could not free the sword. One by one all the knights came forward to try and pull out the sword. And one by one, they failed.

'This is making fools of us all,' said one. 'This is nothing more than some magician's madness. Remember Merlin. He brought us here.'

'Mischief is afoot,' said another. 'We have been summoned here so that the heathen invaders can snatch our lands while our backs are turned.'

'T'is no mischief,' echoed a voice from the dark, green yew tree. The knights looked up and saw the familiar figure of Merlin sitting on a thick bough. 'The sword speaks the truth,' said Merlin. 'And the truth is that the one who will pull out this sword is not here yet. But he will come and you will all witness who God has chosen to be king. And he will be more than King of England; he will become the warrior chief of all Britain. The kings of Scotland, Ireland and Wales will all bow down to him one day.' The next moment Merlin vanished into the depths of the yew, the holiest of all the trees, and disappeared.

'Now, where has that maker of magic gone?' cried King Anguish of Ireland. 'He is nothing but a troublesome sorcerer. Remember how he told us he was a child of the Devil. Come, let's be gone.'

Everyone left the churchyard and returned to their lodgings in the city to warm themselves and begin their Christmas feasting.

Merlin had no time for Christmas celebrations. He was waiting for a young lad to reach the city.

13

The Boy King

Later that Christmas morning, Sir Ector, a knight who had journeyed all the way from the north of England, reached the edge of the city. Riding beside him were his son, Sir Kay, and his foster-son Arthur, a young sixteen year old lad.

As they looked down on the great city, Sir Kay suddenly realised that he had lost his sword. 'Father,' he said, 'I cannot go into the city without my sword. Arthur must hurry back the way we have come and see if he can find it.'

Arthur spurred his horse and rode off to find the sword. But, try as he might to take the road they had come on, the horse would not follow it. Arthur pulled hard on the reins but a stronger force than he was at work. The horse galloped towards the city, only stopping when it reached the churchyard. Arthur spotted the sword in the anvil.

'My prayers are answered,' said Arthur, dismounting and walking over to the stone. It was the finest sword he had ever seen and he knew that his brother would be pleased to have it. Arthur did not see the shadowy figure smiling in the yew tree. He grasped the sword and, with one pull, it was free. He didn't notice the inscription on the blade as he rode back to his father and brother. He found them talking to some other knights.

'Brother, I have found you a wonderful sword,' cried Arthur.

One of the knights with his father gasped when he saw the sword. 'Did you pull it from the anvil in the churchyard?'

'Yes, my Lord,' replied Arthur.

'Then t'is nothing but mischief. You cannot be king,' said the knight.

'Me, a king?' answered a puzzled Arthur.

Sir Ector turned to Arthur. 'There is only one way we can prove this. We must go to this churchyard and see this anvil for ourselves.' They rode into the city and reached the churchyard. Arthur replaced the sword in the anvil and the others were summoned from their lodgings. Many came grumbling that their feast had been interrupted. Once more they all tried to pull out the sword and again they all failed. 'Now Arthur,' said Sir Ector, 'it is your turn.'

Arthur stepped forward and grasped the sword. Everyone watched in silence as his fingers tightened around the hilt. It was done in an instant. The sword slipped from the anvil as easily as a battle-axe from butter. The onlookers gasped. Sir Ector sank to his knees, 'Arthur, you are of more noble blood than I ever thought,' he said.

As they spoke, many of the other knights started to argue among themselves. 'This youngster cannot be king,' said some.

Sir Ector turned to them and said that he believed Arthur was the rightful king. 'But if you still don't believe it, let us return here at the festival of Candlemas and find out who can remove the sword. And between now and then, a guard shall be mounted on the anvil to see that no magic or mischief comes about.'

At Candlemas they returned. Once more Arthur was the only one who could remove the sword. But still some of the lords refused to believe he was meant to be king. Sir Ulfius spoke.

'I, for one, am sure Arthur is the chosen one. But, to convince the doubters, we will all return at Easter.'

Sir Ulfius was so convinced that he, Sir Brastias and Sir Baudwin decided to stay with Arthur to await the final trial. They feared some ambitious warlord might try to kill Arthur. Those three knights, who had all served King Uther so loyally, never let Arthur out of their sight.

The snows had melted and spring buds covered the hedgerows as the kings, knights and nobles returned to London at Easter. The sword had been untouched since Candlemas. The knights tried their luck again, but it was all in vain. Arthur took his turn, but this time Merlin, hiding once more in the yew tree, stretched out his gnarled old fingers and pointed at the sword.

Arthur grasped the sword. A blinding light danced along the length of the blade. The knights cried out with fear and hid their eyes from the dazzling blaze. When they looked again, they saw that Arthur now held the sword aloft.

'Arthur is our chosen king,' bellowed Sir Ulfius. 'No one can deny it now.'

16

Everyone sank to their knees, many begging Arthur to forgive them for ever doubting him.

The church was hurriedly prepared and Uther's crown brought. Arthur was led to the altar. There he was first knighted by Sir Ulfius and then crowned Arthur, King of England.

Afterwards the nervous young man gave everyone a promise. He said that if anyone had lost their lands in battles since Uther's death, they would be returned. 'And if the heathen invaders have robbed you of anything,' he said, 'then I will fight for its return. England will once again be one land and one people.'

King Arthur was escorted to the castle at Camelot. That night he lay awake, worrying about the task ahead. He was so young. How could he bring peace to the kingdom of England? How could he defeat the heathens?

Merlin heard his lonely voice.

The Prophesies of Merlin

King Arthur woke to see a young boy of about fourteen standing at the bottom of his bed. He was about to shout for the guards when he saw that the boy could do no harm. He wasn't even armed with a sword.

'How did you get past the guards?' asked Arthur.

'A child could not … but an enchanter can,' said the boy in a voice which seemed far older than it should be.

'Who are you?' Arthur asked.

'I am who I am … but then again I am not what I am.' Arthur smiled at the strange answer.

'T'is right you smile at me,' said the boy, 'because I come as a friend. I have answers to your puzzles.'

'What puzzles do I have?' asked Arthur.

'Puzzles a plenty,' said the boy. 'You don't know where you have come from. Nor do you know where you are going. But I can tell you. Your father knows why.'

'My father! You don't know who my father was.'

The boy danced around the room. 'Your questions are so easy. Your father, ha! Uther Pendragon, King of all England, was he. And never was there a nobler man. And your mother? Why, she still lives but a child's leap from this room. It is Queen Igraine.'

Arthur did not believe him. 'How can a boy your age tell such things? You are not old enough to have even known who my father was. It's just childish prattle you're speaking.' Arthur became irritated. He told the boy to get out and turned over to go back to sleep. But then he looked up again. The boy had gone, but in his place now stood a wizened old man of nearly eighty years.

'If you don't believe the child in me, will you believe an old man?' said the stranger.

'Who are you?' asked Arthur.

'I am Merlin; a riddler, a fiddler, a magician and meddler. A child of the Devil some say. Yet others know me for the good I do. But ask me no questions today. I have many things to tell you; some which reveal your past and others which show the future and what you must do.'

Arthur listened to every word as Merlin told him that he was, indeed, the son of King Uther and Queen Igraine. The young king was even more surprised when Merlin told him that they had met before.

'But you won't remember because you were a babe in arms,' he explained. 'I knew your father well and often he used my magic to help him. Sir Ulfius, Sir Brastias and Sir Baudwin, they'll tell you it is true.' Merlin told Arthur how England had been in turmoil when he had been born. 'Many men,' he said, 'wanted to steal your father's throne. They would have killed you if they had known you had been born.'

'So what happened to me?' asked Arthur.

Merlin told Arthur he had advised Uther that his newborn son should be taken away and brought up in hiding; a safe place where no one would know the secret of his birth.

'So,' said Merlin, 'I took you as a babe from your mother's arms and carried you myself all the way to Sir Ector's home. I never told Sir Ector who you really were. And I never told Uther or Igraine where you had gone. How they yearned to see you, and how Queen Igraine cried. But I could not allow it.'

'So my father died without knowing what had become of me,' said Arthur.

'No. He knew. I went to him on his death-bed and whispered all. He knew then that you would succeed him as king, and he died happy with my news.'

'And the sword in the anvil?' asked Arthur.

'It was I who set the sacred sword in the anvil,' said Merlin. 'It was I who built the anvil. And it was I who called the knights and nobles to try their hand at the sword. And only I knew that you would be the one to succeed. And now I will be the one to guide and advise you.'

Arthur was a little frightened at all he heard, and still didn't quite believe the strange figure at the end of his bed.

'You may doubt me now,' said Merlin, as if he had heard Arthur's thoughts. 'But you will come to trust me. Today you must ask your mother, Queen Igraine, whether she and Uther had a son. Ask her what happened to him. Then you will know that I speak the truth.'

Merlin sat down on the bed beside Arthur. He had other things to tell the young king. 'One day you will rule not just England, but all of Britain. The kings of Wales, Scotland and Ireland will swear allegiance to you. So too will all the chieftains in this land, from Cornwall in the South to the Orkneys in the North.'

Then Merlin's expression changed. He said that two members of Arthur's own family would try and steal his throne, one by magic, and one by treachery. 'The one who deals in magic,' said Merlin, 'will do all in her power to destroy you. Yet, another even more powerful enchantress will come to help you. She is so powerful that one day she will even steal all my magic and carry me away.'

Arthur wanted to know more. Merlin would only reveal that the king would soon be troubled by the witch, but the traitor would not reveal himself until Arthur was old.

'The traitor will meet you on the battlefield,' said Merlin, 'and that day will see your death.'

The young Arthur shuddered at the words. But Merlin gave him a kindly look and told him not to worry about events which would happen many years in the future. Merlin rose and walked to the door.

'Worry not, King Arthur. You are born to be the greatest King that England ever had.'

Without another word, he was gone. Arthur wasn't sure whether he had gone through the door or simply vanished. Arthur leapt from his bed and hurriedly dressed. Then he ran to Queen Igraine's room. Excitedly, he told her all that Merlin had said. 'Is it true, dear lady?' he asked.

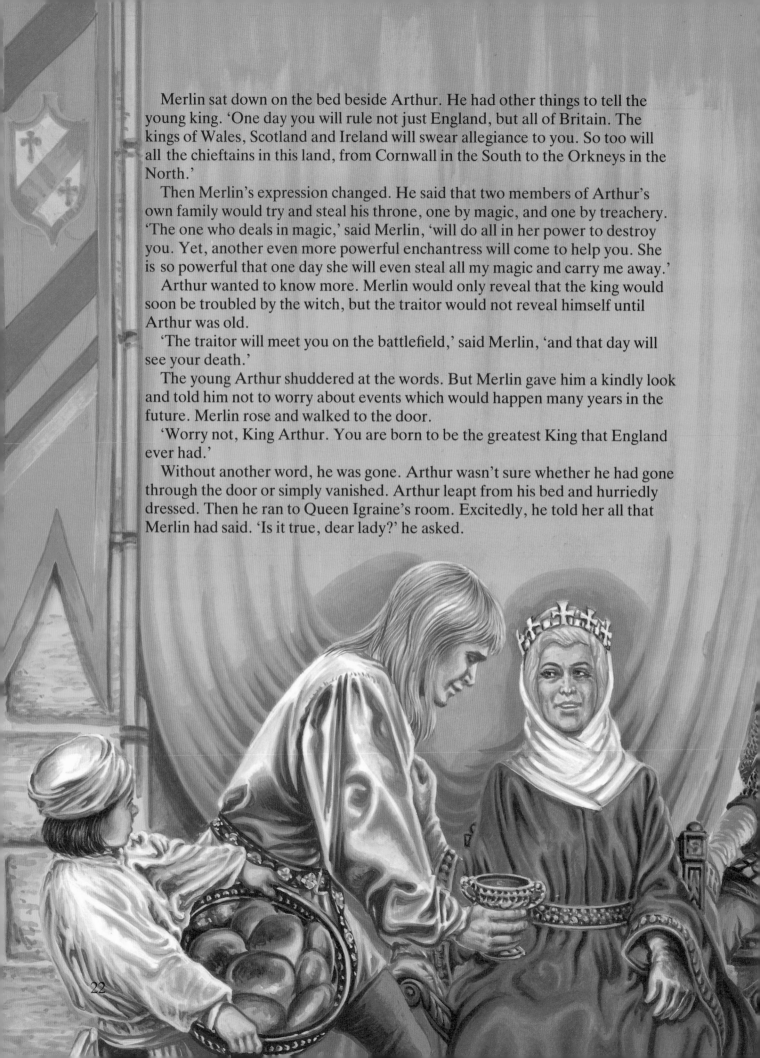

Queen Igraine burst into tears. 'Merlin often helped my dear Uther. Ulfius, Brastias and Baudwin would tell you that. We did have a son, a son so dear to me. Yet Merlin came the day he was born and took him away. I have not seen him since.' Queen Igraine looked deeply into Arthur's eyes. A mother never forgets. She had suspected at first sight that Arthur was the boy who had been taken from her so many years before. 'My son!' she cried.

Arthur fell into his mother's arms and wept.

The celebrations at Camelot continued for a week. Arthur and his mother spent many hours together. But there was also work to be done. Arthur had to set the kingdom in order. He appointed Sir Ulfius as his Lord Chamberlain. Sir Baudwin became Chief Marshall and Sir Brastias, a bold fighter, took responsibility for raising an army for the king.

Camelot was such a happy place that Spring. Yet even as the wild flowers blossomed in the meadows beneath the castle walls, trouble was not far away. Some powerful warlords in the kingdom still refused to believe that young Arthur was their rightful king.

23

Excalibur

It was midsummer when King Arthur left Camelot to visit some of his lands. He reached the town of Caerleon in Wales where a great feast had been arranged in his honour.

Arthur was delighted when he received news that six kings were coming to visit him. Among them were his brothers-in-law, King Lot of Lothian and King Uriens of Gore. They had married Arthur's sisters, Margawse and Morgan Le Fay. He was so happy that he sent out servants to greet them with gifts. He was very surprised when the servants returned with the gifts.

'Why is this?' asked Arthur.

24

One of the servants explained. 'The kings refused your gifts. They say you are not of royal blood and are not the rightful king. They refuse to be ruled by you.'

'What does this mean?' said Arthur.

'They are not coming alone,' said another servant. 'They have thousands of knights. They are determined to kill you and put another on the throne.'

The alarm bells in the city were rung and every able-bodied man was called to arms. But even then Arthur could only muster but a few hundred men to meet the thousands now marching on the town.

As the kings were planning their attack, Merlin suddenly appeared in the middle of them. 'Even if you had a hundred thousand men,' he warned, 'you would not win this day. King Arthur is the true king. So return to your lands and give Arthur your allegiance.'

'What nonsense,' said King Lot, 'I won't listen to the words of an old blustering sorcerer. Be gone!'

But King Lot trembled when Merlin told him he would meet his death if they attacked the town.

Merlin next went to Arthur and told him to open the city gate. Arthur could not believe Merlin's advice. But the wise enchanter insisted. 'Do as I say and place your men on the city walls and on all the city rooftops.'

So the great gate was opened. The kings stared in astonishment.

25

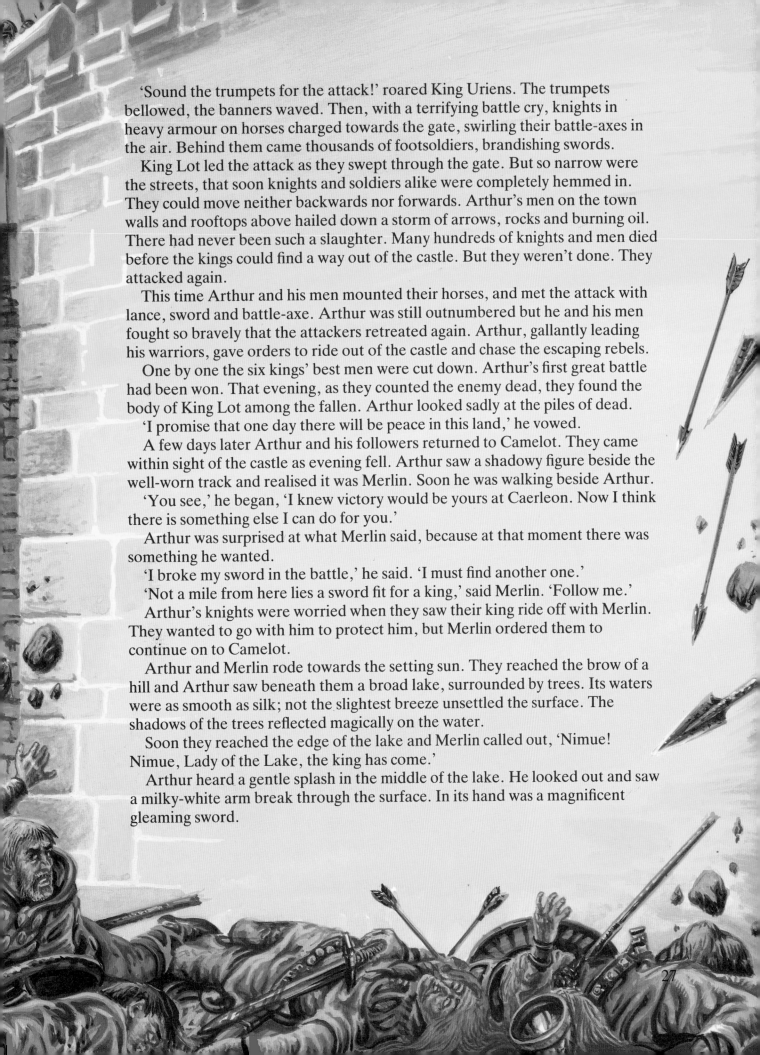

'Sound the trumpets for the attack!' roared King Uriens. The trumpets bellowed, the banners waved. Then, with a terrifying battle cry, knights in heavy armour on horses charged towards the gate, swirling their battle-axes in the air. Behind them came thousands of footsoldiers, brandishing swords.

King Lot led the attack as they swept through the gate. But so narrow were the streets, that soon knights and soldiers alike were completely hemmed in. They could move neither backwards nor forwards. Arthur's men on the town walls and rooftops above hailed down a storm of arrows, rocks and burning oil. There had never been such a slaughter. Many hundreds of knights and men died before the kings could find a way out of the castle. But they weren't done. They attacked again.

This time Arthur and his men mounted their horses, and met the attack with lance, sword and battle-axe. Arthur was still outnumbered but he and his men fought so bravely that the attackers retreated again. Arthur, gallantly leading his warriors, gave orders to ride out of the castle and chase the escaping rebels.

One by one the six kings' best men were cut down. Arthur's first great battle had been won. That evening, as they counted the enemy dead, they found the body of King Lot among the fallen. Arthur looked sadly at the piles of dead.

'I promise that one day there will be peace in this land,' he vowed.

A few days later Arthur and his followers returned to Camelot. They came within sight of the castle as evening fell. Arthur saw a shadowy figure beside the well-worn track and realised it was Merlin. Soon he was walking beside Arthur.

'You see,' he began, 'I knew victory would be yours at Caerleon. Now I think there is something else I can do for you.'

Arthur was surprised at what Merlin said, because at that moment there was something he wanted.

'I broke my sword in the battle,' he said. 'I must find another one.'

'Not a mile from here lies a sword fit for a king,' said Merlin. 'Follow me.'

Arthur's knights were worried when they saw their king ride off with Merlin. They wanted to go with him to protect him, but Merlin ordered them to continue on to Camelot.

Arthur and Merlin rode towards the setting sun. They reached the brow of a hill and Arthur saw beneath them a broad lake, surrounded by trees. Its waters were as smooth as silk; not the slightest breeze unsettled the surface. The shadows of the trees reflected magically on the water.

Soon they reached the edge of the lake and Merlin called out, 'Nimue! Nimue, Lady of the Lake, the king has come.'

Arthur heard a gentle splash in the middle of the lake. He looked out and saw a milky-white arm break through the surface. In its hand was a magnificent gleaming sword.

'There's your blade,' said Merlin. 'It's called Excalibur.'

Suddenly Arthur felt the presence of someone nearby. He looked all about him but could see nothing but mists which were creeping around the lake's edge. Then out of the mist came a barge carrying the most beautiful lady he had ever seen.

'Merlin,' said Arthur, a little frightened at the strange figure. 'Who is she?'

'Nimue, the Lady of the Lake,' said Merlin. 'I have spoken to you about her already. She will be your guardian in some of your troubles ahead. And it is her beauty which will soon steal my magic and take me away from you.'

The barge drifted into the bank in front of Arthur. The lady looked closely at Arthur but did not say a word. It was Arthur who spoke first.

'Whose sword is that?' he asked, pointing to the blade still flashing in the middle of the lake. 'I have need of one.'

'It is mine,' said Nimue, the Lady of the Lake. 'And for a promise it will be yours.'

Arthur promised that he would give her anything she asked. The Lady of the Lake beckoned Arthur to join her in the barge. No sooner was he aboard, than it moved away, as if powered by some secret force. It glided out to where the mysterious arm still held the sword aloft. Arthur's eyes opened wide when he saw the sword. Its hilt was decorated with gold and precious stones. And the blade gave off a dazzling light. He grasped it with both hands and lifted it into the air. The arm which had held it slipped beneath the surface of the water and vanished.

The barge floated back to the shore where Merlin was waiting.

'It is the finest sword that I have ever seen,' said Arthur. 'But what promise must I make?'

'Promise me,' said Nimue, 'that when you die, you will return Excalibur to me.'

Arthur gave her his promise as the barge moved away. In a moment it had disappeared into the mists again.

'Excalibur is no ordinary sword,' said Merlin, as they rode away from the enchanted lake. 'It will protect you. Whenever it is with you, you and your kingdom will be safe. But be warned that without it, your life will be in much danger. Keep it by your side always.'

There was bad news for King Arthur when he reached Camelot again. The five kings who had survived the Battle of Caerleon had joined forces with five more kings and were marching south. Arthur sent out spies and they reported that the kings were coming with tens of thousands of men-at-arms.

'We are doomed,' said Arthur. 'They will overrun us. We cannot match their forces.'

Merlin appeared at his side once more. 'Prepare for battle,' he said. 'Victory will be yours. You will see. Now, I must be away. I have work to do.'

Arthur called his warrior knights together and told them what Merlin had said. Many were worried because Arthur only had but a few hundred men. But wise Sir Ulfius calmed everyone.

'Put your trust in Merlin,' he said. 'With Merlin on our side, we will win the battle.'

Sir Brastias agreed. 'Soon comes the eve of Hallowe'en. My Lord, you must choose that day to fight.'

'Why Hallowe'en?' asked Arthur.

'T'is the night when ghosts and hobgoblins are about,' said Sir Baudwin. 'It is Merlin's night.'

Arthur marched out his few hundred men and took up a position on a hill with a great forest at his back. Day by day he looked down and saw his enemies preparing for battle. Never had such a large army come together.

Days passed and there was still no sign of Merlin. At last the Eve of Hallowe'en arrived and Arthur knew the battle could be delayed no longer. He called on his knights to prepare to fight at sunset.

The kings in the valley below laughed when they saw Arthur's few hundred men mount their horses. 'It will be over at the first charge,' they laughed.

Arthur lined up his knights and took his place at the front. 'Sound the trumpets,' he cried. 'May God and his miracles be with us in battle.'

The trumpets blasted out and Arthur and his knights rode down the hill, first at a trot, then a canter and finally a full gallop. The rebel kings' men waited for the attack, protected by lines of thick stakes sharpened to a point. They were sure Arthur's men and horses would all be impaled on the deadly stakes.

But the gallant knights flew down the hill like the wind and, when they reached the lines of stakes, they jumped right over them, striking out at the enemy with their swords. The speed of the charge carried King Arthur's men right through the enemy lines and up the other side of the valley. Once more they charged into the attack, leaping over the enemy, striking a thousand blows with swords and battle-axes.

Arthur looked down and saw that the attacks had surprised the ten kings. He lined up his knights and prepared to attack again. He was almost ready to give the order to charge when he heard a strange sound coming from the forest behind him. It sounded like a roll of approaching thunder. Arthur looked back but he could see nothing in the darkness.

Sir Ulfius saw him looking back and called out, 'Don't worry, my Lord, remember this is Hallowe'en. Many strange creatures are about, come we must attack again.'

The trumpets sounded and Arthur's men swept down the hill again. Hardly had the horses reached a canter when Arthur heard another trumpet call and saw the most amazing sight.

The enemy were fleeing, scampering away in every direction. Arthur could not understand it, until he looked back in the direction from where the second trumpet call had come.

'Ye Gods,' cried Arthur, seeing tens of thousands of men bursting out from the forest. And there, sitting high in a tree, was Merlin.

'I've brought you an army,' he cried. 'Charge again. Victory is yours.'

Arthur and his knights galloped down the hill with Merlin's men behind them. The battle was quick and bloody. The rebels were slaughtered and the killing only stopped when King Arthur cried out to the kings to lay down their arms and surrender.

'Why are we fighting each other,' said King Arthur, 'when our real enemy, the heathens are pillaging our lands? They will destroy us unless we fight together. United we will sweep them from our country.'

At last the ten kings saw the truth and, one by one, came forward and swore allegiance to King Arthur, promising to fight for him against the heathens. Just then two more kings in full battle armour rode up and dismounted. They knelt before King Arthur.

'Sir, we served your father well,' said the first, 'and today we have had the honour to battle for his son.'

Arthur was confused, but Merlin came to explain. 'When I left you I went to France to seek help from your father's most loyal allies. These men are King Ban of Benwick and King Bors of Gaul. It was their armies which came to win this day with you.'

Arthur warmly embraced the two kings from France and ordered that a great feast be prepared to celebrate the day. That night Arthur shared his table with not just the two French kings, but the ten others who were now his sworn allies and loyal servants.

And so Arthur became King of Britain. In the months ahead he led his armies against the heathen warriors. Twelve great battles he fought, and twelve times he was victorious.

Arthur, King of all Britain, had won his kingdom.

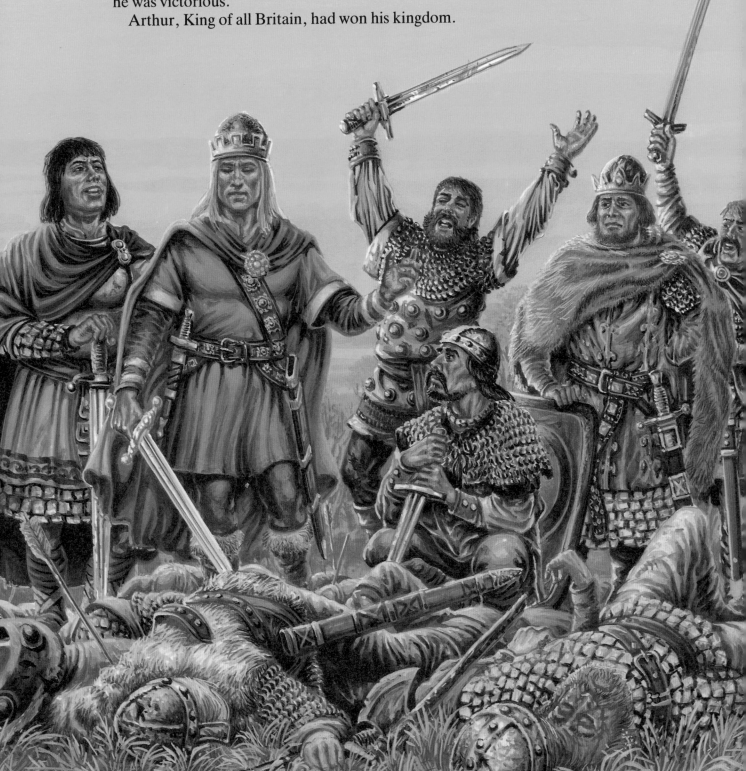

Arthur Marries Guinevere

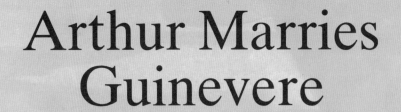

Britain was at peace at last and the time had come for King Arthur to choose a queen. Arthur had long known who he wanted to marry. He had met her during his battles against the heathens. His army had gone to help King Leodegrance of Cameliard. The king had a daughter called Guinevere, a great beauty. Arthur had fallen in love with her at first sight.

Once again Arthur sought advice from Merlin. 'My people say I should marry,' he said. 'There is but one for me. Guinevere, the daughter of King Leodegrance. He was a great friend of my father and this marriage will strengthen the bonds between our families.'

'She is of matchless beauty, perhaps the most beautiful lady alive,' said

34

Merlin. 'Yet, I still say you should not marry her.'

'Why not?' said Arthur. 'She is of royal blood herself. There can be no better match for me. She will be my queen.'

Merlin replied in a hushed voice. 'I have proved to you that I can see the future, and I will give you another glimpse of what is to come. Guinevere is meant for another. One day a knight - the most courageous and bold - will win her heart. The future cannot be changed. She will love another person one day.'

Arthur would not listen. His heart was set on marrying Guinevere. There was nothing that Merlin could say to change his mind.

'So be it,' said Merlin, as he departed. 'But one day you will remember my warning.'

Merlin went to King Leodegrance and told him that Arthur wanted to marry his daughter. The king was delighted. Arthur could not have given him a higher honour.

'Guinevere will be his queen,' said the king, 'and to mark this great day I shall give noble Arthur the most precious of gifts. Come my merry wizard, methinks you know well what it is.'

35

The king led Merlin into a great hall and there, in the middle of the room, was a huge table. Its legs were as thick as a man's body and they supported a huge circular table-top large enough to seat a hundred and fifty people.

'This shall be their wedding gift,' said the king. 'It was given to me by King Arthur's father, Uther Pendragon himself.'

Merlin recognised the table instantly.

'There can be no better gift,' he said, 'for it is written in the future that this table will play its part in the life of Arthur, King of the Britons. You know well, King Leodegrance, that with my own magic I built it.'

'And with this gift,' said the king, 'I shall send a hundred knights to fight for Arthur. Each one will have a seat at the table.'

And so the marriage was arranged. A great procession left Cameliard. The king with his daughter, Guinevere, rode at the head of a long column of men and wagons. The Round Table itself was so large that it had been taken apart in pieces and now a dozen wagons carried it southwards. At the rear came King Leodegrance's one hundred knights.

When they reached the court at Camelot, Arthur was so happy to see everyone arrive. But he was even more pleased when he saw what King Leodegrance had brought him.

The table was put together in the Great Hall at Camelot. King Leodegrance's knights were the first to take their place, each seat was inscribed with the name of the man who sat there. Then it was the turn of King Arthur's knights.

Merlin appeared beside the table. 'In times to come, all these seats will be filled by bold and brave knights; famous knights of whom all the world will hear tell.'

Arthur noticed two empty places; one was unmarked but the other beside it was inscribed with the words: SIEGE PERILOUS. He asked Merlin who would sit in the two seats. 'One day the bravest and most courageous knight of all will sit in the unmarked chair,' said Merlin, 'and beware of the second one, the Siege Perilous. Let no man sit there. That seat belongs to the most Christian knight. He has yet to be born. His place must remain empty until he is brought to your court. Anyone who sits in his seat does so at their peril.'

Arthur promised that no person would sit there until the day came.

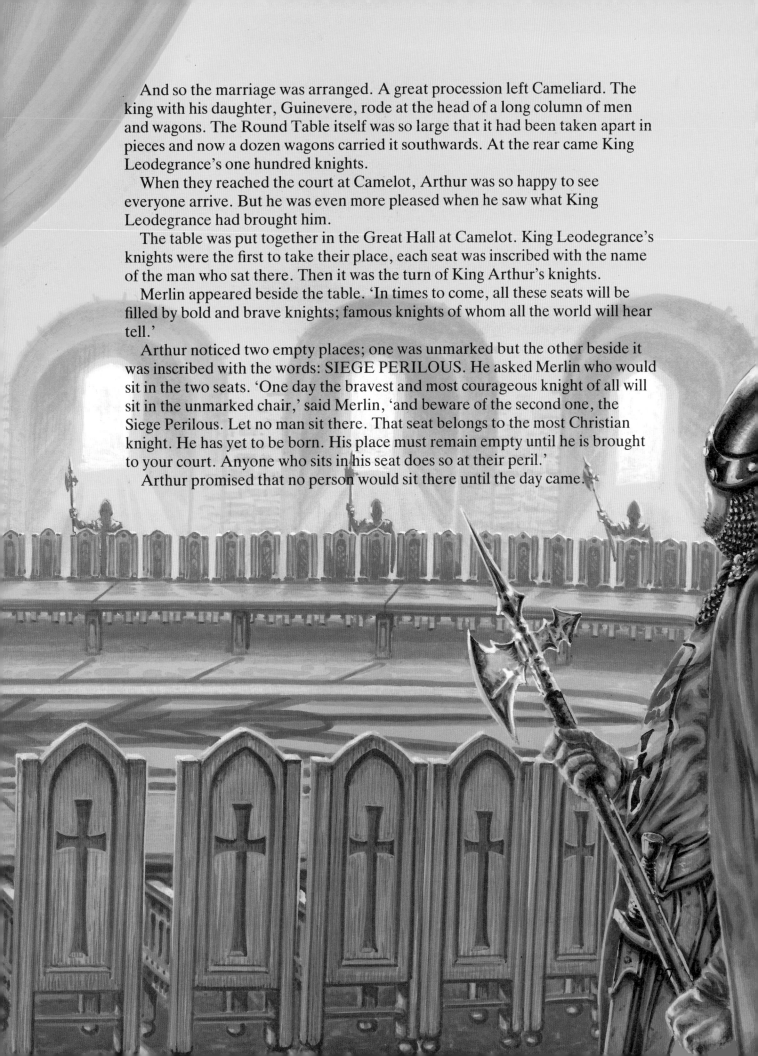

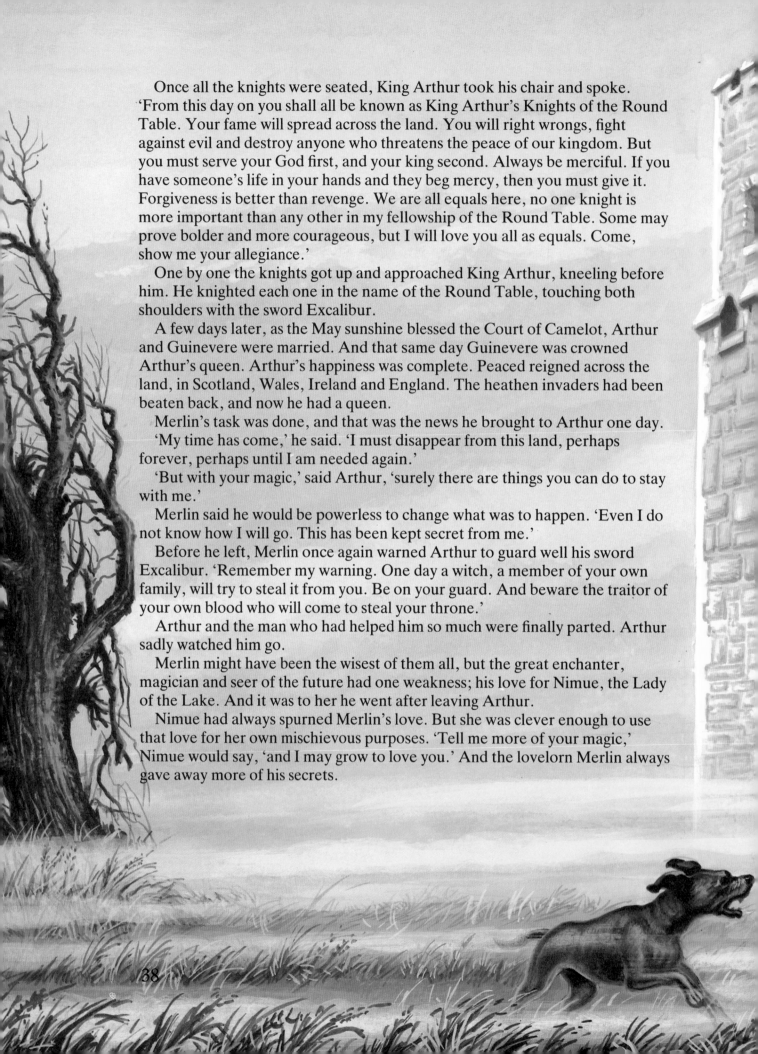

Once all the knights were seated, King Arthur took his chair and spoke. 'From this day on you shall all be known as King Arthur's Knights of the Round Table. Your fame will spread across the land. You will right wrongs, fight against evil and destroy anyone who threatens the peace of our kingdom. But you must serve your God first, and your king second. Always be merciful. If you have someone's life in your hands and they beg mercy, then you must give it. Forgiveness is better than revenge. We are all equals here, no one knight is more important than any other in my fellowship of the Round Table. Some may prove bolder and more courageous, but I will love you all as equals. Come, show me your allegiance.'

One by one the knights got up and approached King Arthur, kneeling before him. He knighted each one in the name of the Round Table, touching both shoulders with the sword Excalibur.

A few days later, as the May sunshine blessed the Court of Camelot, Arthur and Guinevere were married. And that same day Guinevere was crowned Arthur's queen. Arthur's happiness was complete. Peaced reigned across the land, in Scotland, Wales, Ireland and England. The heathen invaders had been beaten back, and now he had a queen.

Merlin's task was done, and that was the news he brought to Arthur one day.

'My time has come,' he said. 'I must disappear from this land, perhaps forever, perhaps until I am needed again.'

'But with your magic,' said Arthur, 'surely there are things you can do to stay with me.'

Merlin said he would be powerless to change what was to happen. 'Even I do not know how I will go. This has been kept secret from me.'

Before he left, Merlin once again warned Arthur to guard well his sword Excalibur. 'Remember my warning. One day a witch, a member of your own family, will try to steal it from you. Be on your guard. And beware the traitor of your own blood who will come to steal your throne.'

Arthur and the man who had helped him so much were finally parted. Arthur sadly watched him go.

Merlin might have been the wisest of them all, but the great enchanter, magician and seer of the future had one weakness; his love for Nimue, the Lady of the Lake. And it was to her he went after leaving Arthur.

Nimue had always spurned Merlin's love. But she was clever enough to use that love for her own mischievous purposes. 'Tell me more of your magic,' Nimue would say, 'and I may grow to love you.' And the lovelorn Merlin always gave away more of his secrets.

Some said Merlin should have used his own magic to win her heart. But the enchantress had seen to that. She had made Merlin make a solemn vow that he would never use his magic on her. He had gladly promised in the hope that one day she would be his.

In time Merlin revealed to her all the magic he knew, everything, that is, except the mysteries of the enchanted cavern by the lake where the Lady of the Lake lived.

But love was not on Merlin's mind when he visited her this time. Merlin knew that there was one more task he had to do if the story of King Arthur was to unfold as he foretold.

Merlin and the Lady of the Lake journeyed to Benwick in France and the court of King Ban. He had helped Arthur win his great battle against the ten kings. The king's wife had just had a baby son and they had named him Lancelot.

Merlin cradled the boy in his arms as he spoke with King Ban. 'This is the boy who will grow up to become the bravest and most courageous knight who ever sat at King Arthur's Round Table. It is written that he must be brought up by the Lady of the Lake. We must take him now.'

King Ban knew Merlin well enough to know that his advice must be followed. With tears in his eyes, he gave the baby Lancelot to the Lady of the Lake. Merlin and Nimue travelled back to the lake, where Lancelot was put into the care of Nimue's maidservants.

That night the Lady of the Lake finally persuaded Merlin to show her what mysteries lay inside the enchanted cavern. 'You shall win my heart for it,' she smiled.

Merlin, the foolish lover, could not resist. At the rock he cast a spell and a huge stone rolled away, revealing a dark cavern beneath.

40

'Come, show me what's inside,' she begged.

Merlin disappeared into the darkness, beckoning her to follow.

As soon as he was deep inside, she cast a powerful spell. The rock rolled back across the entrance, leaving Merlin trapped inside.

The Lady of the Lake left as Merlin tried all his magic to remove the stone. But his powers had gone. She had stolen all of them and now Merlin was doomed to stay in his lake side prison.

That night Sir Bagdemagus, a Knight of the Round Table, rode past and heard Merlin's laments echoing from beneath the great rock. When Merlin realised he was there, he told him to leave. 'There is nothing you can do,' he said sadly. 'My task is done. I must stay here until I am needed again. Only Nimue can free me now.'

Sir Bagdemagus rode off as Merlin's cries grew louder and louder.

Morgan the Sister Witch

One day King Arthur's youngest sister, Morgan Le Fay, arrived at Camelot with her husband, King Uriens of Gore. He had fought against Arthur in his early days, but now he was a loyal subject.

'Greetings, brother,' said Morgan, her long, jet black hair blowing in the wind.

Arthur had never known his youngest sister very well. He had been told horrifying stories about her; that she could talk to the dead and cast terrible spells. Some said she had come from the kingdom of the spirits.

The next day Arthur arranged a hunt. At dawn all the Knights of the Round Table rode out. They soon caught the scent of a deer and the horsemen gave chase. What a beast it was. It was so fleet of foot that soon only Arthur, King Uriens and Sir Accolon of Gaul were left in the chase.

Over hill and dale they raced, but the deer never tired. Soon King Arthur and his companions were separated from the main group of huntsmen. Arthur would not give up. Ever onward he urged his horse and the other two followed.

As evening fell the deer led the gallant three towards the setting sun, their horses panting hard. It had been such a long chase that the horses, exhausted, dropped dead beneath their riders. Arthur, Sir Accolon and King Uriens were thrown clear, but still they refused to give up the chase. The deer had slowed down and the hunters took after it on foot.

It was as if the deer was leading them on, slowing when the hunters slowed, going faster when they came close. Suddenly they saw the deer disappear over a bank. When they reached the spot they saw in the gloomy light that the deer was lying dead on a river-bank. Arthur said they should find somewhere to sleep for the night and carry the beast back to Camelot in the morning.

At that moment the mists on the river lifted. A ship appeared. Slowly it drifted into the river-bank.

'It's a ghost ship,' said King Uriens. 'Let's get away.'

43

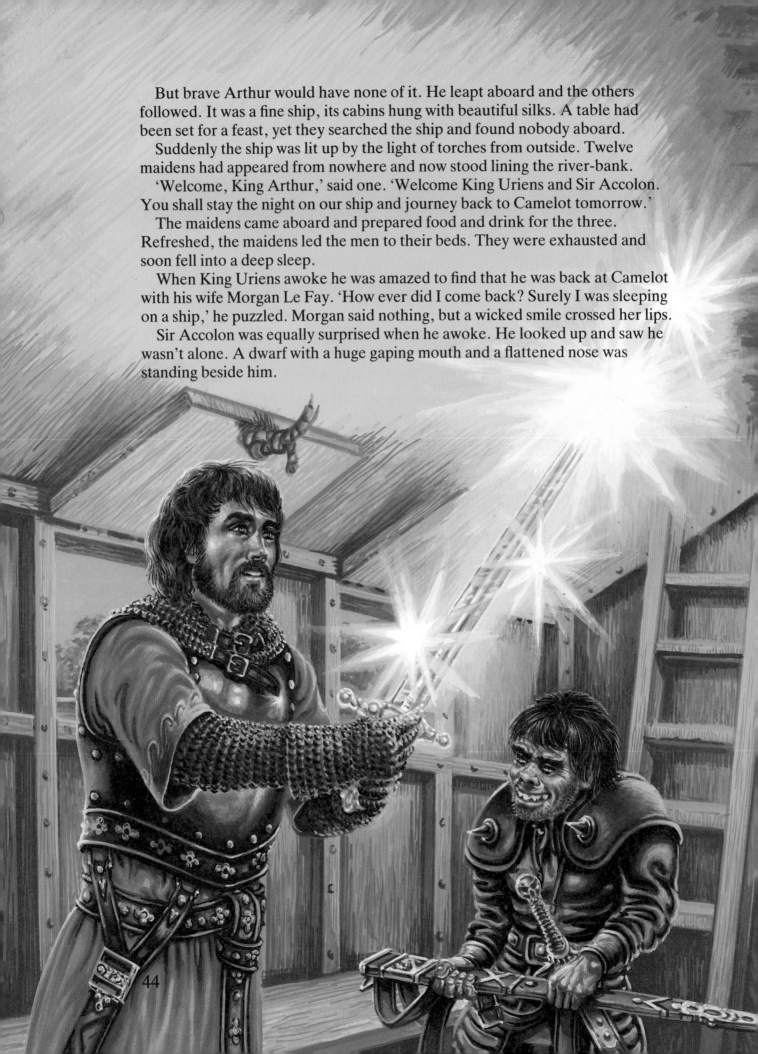

But brave Arthur would have none of it. He leapt aboard and the others
followed. It was a fine ship, its cabins hung with beautiful silks. A table had
been set for a feast, yet they searched the ship and found nobody aboard.

Suddenly the ship was lit up by the light of torches from outside. Twelve
maidens had appeared from nowhere and now stood lining the river-bank.

'Welcome, King Arthur,' said one. 'Welcome King Uriens and Sir Accolon.
You shall stay the night on our ship and journey back to Camelot tomorrow.'

The maidens came aboard and prepared food and drink for the three.
Refreshed, the maidens led the men to their beds. They were exhausted and
soon fell into a deep sleep.

When King Uriens awoke he was amazed to find that he was back at Camelot
with his wife Morgan Le Fay. 'How ever did I come back? Surely I was sleeping
on a ship,' he puzzled. Morgan said nothing, but a wicked smile crossed her lips.

Sir Accolon was equally surprised when he awoke. He looked up and saw he
wasn't alone. A dwarf with a huge gaping mouth and a flattened nose was
standing beside him.

44

'Good morning, noble Sir Accolon,' said the ugly creature. 'I have come from Morgan Le Fay. She sends greetings and begs your help.'

Sir Accolon, feeling as if he had been enchanted by some strange power, replied that if King Arthur's sister wanted his help, then he would give it.

'It is a noble deed she asks,' said the dwarf. 'Look, she has even sent you Arthur's great sword Excalibur to help you in your task.'

'What must I do?' asked Sir Accolon, handling the precious blade in delight.

The dwarf explained that he must fight with an evil knight who would appear the next morning. 'Morgan Le Fay says that you must show him no mercy, as is the usual custom. Even if you have wounded him and he begs for his life, you must take it. These are my mistress's orders.'

'I shall obey,' said Sir Accolon.

When King Arthur woke his comfortable berth on the ship had been exchanged for a dark and damp dungeon. Freezing cold water dripped from the roof. In the dim light he could see that he was not alone. There were other knights in the ghoulish place, some crying out in misery and some dying from hunger. In one corner were the bodies of those who had already died.

'What place is this?' asked Arthur.

'We don't know,' replied one. 'Some say this is the castle of a terrible witch. All we know is that we will all die here.'

Arthur looked around. There was no door. But high up on one of the walls was an opening. A feeble beam of light filtered down. Arthur saw it was impossible for a man to reach the opening. The rocky walls were too smooth and slippery.

Suddenly a figure appeared at the opening. It was a damsel and she called out to King Arthur, 'Good knight, you will not stay here long if you grant me one favour.'

'What is it?' said Arthur.

'There is a knight who comes here tomorrow,' she replied. 'His purpose is to kill my master. Yet he is too old to fight. If you promise to fight this knight, you shall be free.'

'I will do this thing for you, but only if the other knights here are freed with me.'

'It shall be,' said the damsel.

Just then Arthur felt for his sword Excalibur. It had gone. Arthur remembered Merlin's prophesy and recalled how he had said that one of his own family would steal it one day. Arthur looked up at the damsel and felt sure he recognised her. 'Have you ever been to the court of King Arthur? Aren't you a servant of Morgan Le Fay?' he asked.

46

'Never,' she lied. 'And I know of no Morgan Le Fay. Now come, Sir, prepare yourself for the morning when this knight will arrive. I shall provide a horse and armour and your sword will be returned to you.'

Arthur heaved a sigh of relief when he heard Excalibur was not lost forever.

Next morning the damsel appeared again and dropped down a rope ladder. Arthur climbed up, promising the other knights that he would return to free them. A horse and armour had been prepared, and Arthur was already mounted when the damsel brought his sword. Arthur happily grasped Excalibur. Now he was ready to fight any man.

She led Arthur to a nearby field where another knight on horse back was waiting. Both knights' faces were well hidden by their helmets, but beside the other knight stood an ugly dwarf, who suddenly pointed at Arthur.

'That's the man you must kill,' he shrieked.

At the same moment the damsel cried to Arthur, 'That is the knight you must fight.'

The king and the knight did not hesitate. They galloped at each other, their swords ready to strike. They came together like thunder and lightning, both men striking blows so powerful that they were thrown from their horses. Quickly recovering, they ran at each other, slashing and parrying. Each landed many blows on the other, but it was Sir Accolon's cuts which brought first blood. Arthur's blows seemed to have little effect on his opponent.

'What mystery is this?' thought Arthur. 'This sword I carry looks like Excalibur. But I swear it isn't. Some devil has made it to look like my famous blade.'

47

Sir Accolon attacked again. Arthur saw his attacker's sword flashing with the light of thirty torches.

'Treachery,' he cried. 'That is Excalibur.'

'You are right,' said Sir Accolon, still not recognising his lord and king. 'And it will be the death of you.'

Sir Accolon struck again. Arthur was badly wounded, blood pouring from several open cuts. He grew weaker at each step. At last Sir Accolon pierced Arthur's hand. The king's sword fell to the ground.

'I cannot give you mercy,' said Sir Accolon. 'My mistress Morgan Le Fay says you must die.'

'Morgan Le Fay!' cried Arthur, realising at last how he had been tricked. 'Merlin's prophesy has come true.' Indeed it had, yet so too would another part of his prophesy. Merlin had always said that when he had gone another would take his place to guard the king.

Sir Accolon raised Excalibur and was about to strike the fatal blow when Nimue, the Lady of the Lake arrived. She too knew what treachery had been done that day and how Morgan Le Fay had planned Arthur's death so that her husband, King Uriens, could claim his crown.

As Accolon's sword swung down towards Arthur's neck, the Lady of the Lake used her magic. The blade spun out of his hands and flew high into the air. Arthur caught it as it fell to earth.

'Now rogue knight,' cried Arthur. 'Let us see what the real Excalibur can do.'

Arthur leapt to his feet and struck Accolon a tremendous blow, knocking his helmet right off his head. 'What!' cried Arthur, removing his own helmet. 'You are Sir Accolon.'

'My Lord,' said Accolon, recognising King Arthur. 'We have surely been enchanted by some devilish magic. And I think I know who.'

Accolon explained to Arthur how Morgan Le Fay's dwarf had brought him Excalibur. 'He told me she wanted me to fight a knight to the death. But how was I to know it was you. Forgive me, my Lord.'

King Arthur wept when he saw that Excalibur had given Sir Accolon a fatal wound. 'You are not to blame, Sir Accolon,' he said. 'I now know my sister for what she is: a terrible sorceress.'

With that, Sir Accolon died. Arthur returned to the castle where he had been imprisoned and freed the knights in the dungeon. Then he ordered them to carry Sir Accolon's body back to Camelot. 'Tell Morgan Le Fay that her plot is discovered,' said Arthur, 'and warn her that Excalibur is with me once again.'

Arthur did not to return to Camelot. Instead he found his way to an abbey. There he rested and waited for his wounds to heal.

When Sir Accolon's body reached Camelot, Morgan Le Fay asked the knights about Arthur. 'I have not seen my brother for days,' she said, 'I feel sure he, like Sir Accolon, is dead. I shall weep for my poor brother.'

'He is not dead, my lady,' said one of the knights. 'He is badly wounded, but he is recovering in a nearby abbey.'

Morgan Le Fay's face turned ashen. She knew her magic had been destroyed by someone with a greater power. Now her plot was uncovered. She hurried to her husband, King Uriens, and said they must leave immediately.

So Morgan Le Fay left Camelot and returned to her own castle. There she ordered the gate shut and the guards doubled. She was afraid Arthur would take his revenge. She could never be sure that her magic could match that of the person who had helped her brother. But still she plotted King Arthur's death.

Soon after, Arthur returned to Camelot. A few days later a damsel arrived at the court. 'I am from Morgan Le Fay,' she told Arthur. 'My mistress wishes to be forgiven for all she has done. She sends this cloak as a token of her love for you.'

It was the finest cloak that Arthur had ever seen. He admired the hundreds of gems which covered it. 'It is a fine gift,' said Arthur, 'and I would dearly love to forgive my sister.'

Just then Nimue appeared in the court. 'It would be unwise to wear that cloak,' she warned Arthur. 'Instead, let Morgan Le Fay's damsel try it on.'

Arthur knew she was a wise adviser and told the damsel to put the cloak on.

'But I cannot wear a king's cloak,' begged the girl.

'Put it on,' said Arthur.

The damsel slipped the cloak on. Immediately it burst into flames and in a flash the damsel was reduced to a pile of ashes on the floor.

Arthur swore to take his revenge on his evil sister, but Morgan Le Fay could never be caught. Arthur followed her from castle to castle and country to country, but as soon as he caught a glance of her flowing black hair, Morgan disappeared.

The truth was that Arthur often came very close to catching his sister witch. But as soon as she saw him. She always cast her most powerful spell and turned herself into a rock.

Lancelot

The years passed and the Knights of the Round Table became famous for their deeds of bravery. One day Nimue brought a young noble of about fifteen years old to Camelot. He begged King Arthur to make him a knight.

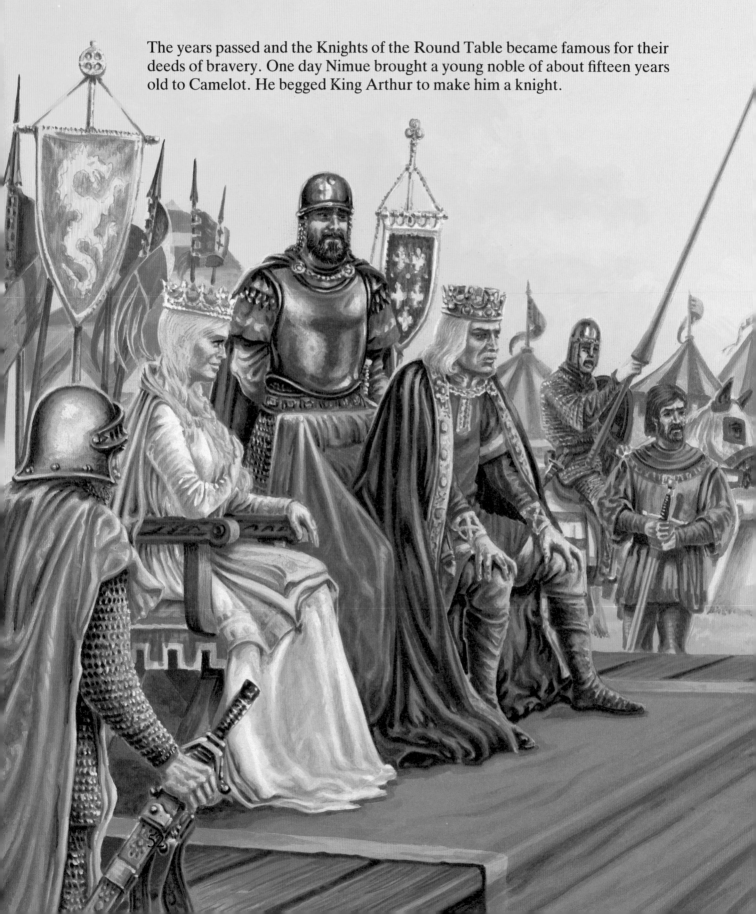

52

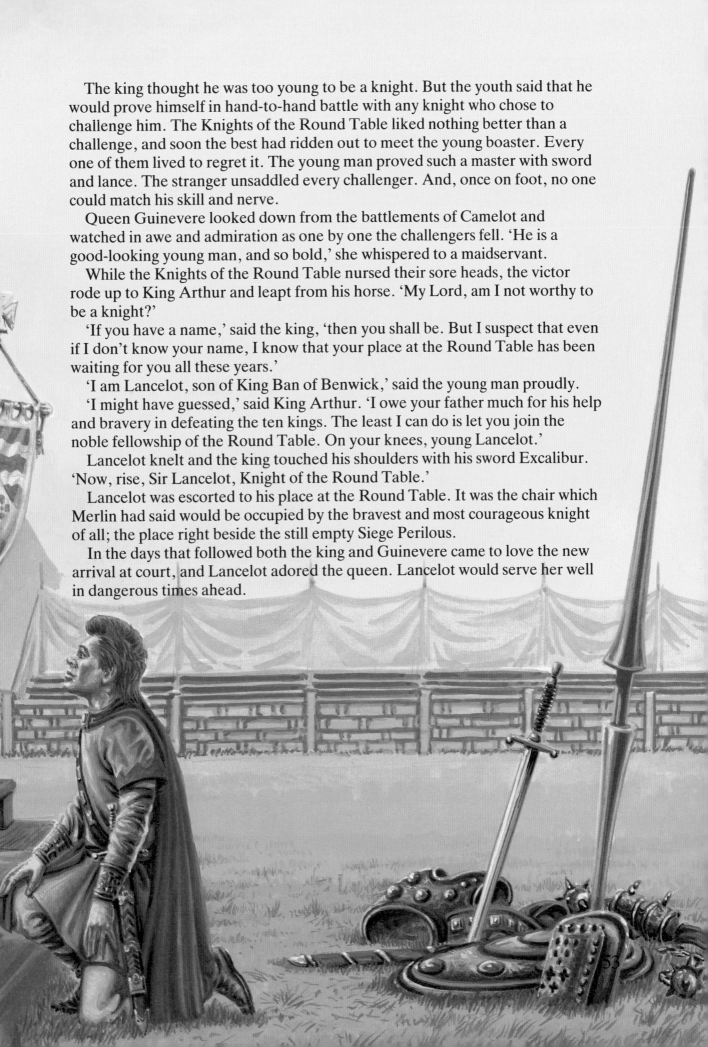

The king thought he was too young to be a knight. But the youth said that he would prove himself in hand-to-hand battle with any knight who chose to challenge him. The Knights of the Round Table liked nothing better than a challenge, and soon the best had ridden out to meet the young boaster. Every one of them lived to regret it. The young man proved such a master with sword and lance. The stranger unsaddled every challenger. And, once on foot, no one could match his skill and nerve.

Queen Guinevere looked down from the battlements of Camelot and watched in awe and admiration as one by one the challengers fell. 'He is a good-looking young man, and so bold,' she whispered to a maidservant.

While the Knights of the Round Table nursed their sore heads, the victor rode up to King Arthur and leapt from his horse. 'My Lord, am I not worthy to be a knight?'

'If you have a name,' said the king, 'then you shall be. But I suspect that even if I don't know your name, I know that your place at the Round Table has been waiting for you all these years.'

'I am Lancelot, son of King Ban of Benwick,' said the young man proudly.

'I might have guessed,' said King Arthur. 'I owe your father much for his help and bravery in defeating the ten kings. The least I can do is let you join the noble fellowship of the Round Table. On your knees, young Lancelot.'

Lancelot knelt and the king touched his shoulders with his sword Excalibur. 'Now, rise, Sir Lancelot, Knight of the Round Table.'

Lancelot was escorted to his place at the Round Table. It was the chair which Merlin had said would be occupied by the bravest and most courageous knight of all; the place right beside the still empty Siege Perilous.

In the days that followed both the king and Guinevere came to love the new arrival at court, and Lancelot adored the queen. Lancelot would serve her well in dangerous times ahead.

53

But Lancelot had a wild and free spirit. He liked nothing better than to roam the country looking for danger, righting wrongs and helping people in trouble. He became famed for his courage.

One day he rode out in search of adventure. He had heard that a murderous knight called Sir Turquin had recently captured some of King Arthur's knights and thrown them into his dungeon. After riding for several hours, Lancelot came across a knight riding by. A wounded knight was straddled across the back of his horse.

'Your name, Sir,' called Lancelot.

'None other than Sir Turquin,' came the haughty reply. 'And who are you who dares to ask my name?'

Lancelot did not answer. He was looking at the wounded man. It was Sir Gaheris, brother of Gawain, the youngest knight of the Round Table.

'You are a scoundrel,' roared Lancelot, his blood boiling with anger. He realised that Gaheris, wounded as he was, was being taken to join the others in Turquin's dungeon. 'How many of King Arthur's knights have you?'

'More than sixty,' laughed Turquin. 'And that dungeon is where they will stay unless you care to fight me for them. If I win, I shall have your life. If you win, they will be freed. But don't think you will escape this with your life. There is only one of King Arthur's knights who could give me any sport.'

'And who is that?' asked Lancelot.

'Sir Lancelot,' said Turquin. 'Yet, I doubt he would trouble me for long.'

'Dismount and look to your sword,' thundered Lancelot.

A moment later the two knights were slashing at each other with their swords and battle-axes. It was violent and bloody, each man receiving deep wounds. They fought on for many hours, neither being able to strike a fatal blow. There was a moment when they stopped to draw breath and Sir Turquin asked Lancelot for his name.

'This bloody fight should have proved who I am,' replied the Knight of the Round Table.

It suddenly dawned on Sir Turquin. 'Sir Lancelot!' he cried, charging at his enemy with greater force than ever.

But Sir Lancelot was ready for him. The good knight's blade slipped past Turquin's guard and pierced his chest.

'You win your wager, Lancelot,' sighed Sir Turquin, slumping to the ground. 'As for me, I shall find new sport in Hell itself.' And with those words, Turquin breathed his last.

Lancelot went and spoke to the wounded Sir Gaheris. 'Gather your strength and ride to Turquin's castle and tell all that Sir Turquin has lost his wager. The Knights of the Round Table must be freed.'

Sir Gaheris mounted his horse and set off for the castle. Lancelot would not go with him. Instead he rode off, restless as ever, for another challenge.

That night the doors to Turquin's dungeon were thrown open and the knights were freed. Among them were Sir Gawain, his brother Sir Agravain and Sir Kay, the king's foster-brother. Sir Kay rode off alone to find Lancelot and thank him.

Lancelot had reached the top of a hill when he saw Sir Kay galloping along the valley beneath him. Suddenly three robbers dashed out of a wood and attacked Sir Kay.

56

Sir Kay was not renowned as a fighter and Lancelot knew that he would be killed. He raced down the hill, his sword whirling in the air. The three men recognised Sir Lancelot and flew off in a cloud of dust. Lancelot let them go and went to help Sir Kay, who had been wounded. That night they stayed in a local inn. Lancelot was up early the next day ready for more mischief.

Sir Kay was still asleep, and, while he slept, Lancelot dressed himself, not in his own armour, but Sir Kay's. Then he leapt onto Sir Kay's horse and rode out. It wasn't long before he saw Sir Gawain and two other Knights of the Round Table on their way back to Camelot. They saw him too.

'Look, that knight wears the armour of Sir Kay,' said Sir Gawain. 'He must have killed Kay.'

All three charged at Lancelot, whose face was hidden by his helmet. But they were no match for his skill. Lancelot rode around them in circles and it only took him a minute to dump all three on the ground.

As he rode off, Sir Gawain spoke. 'We might not have recognised him for his helmet, but there is only one man who could have put us on the floor so easily. That was Sir Lancelot to be sure.'

Lancelot rode back to Sir Kay and they laughed long about how the three knights had been fooled. Lancelot did not stay long. He exchanged his armour, wished Sir Kay well and rode off.

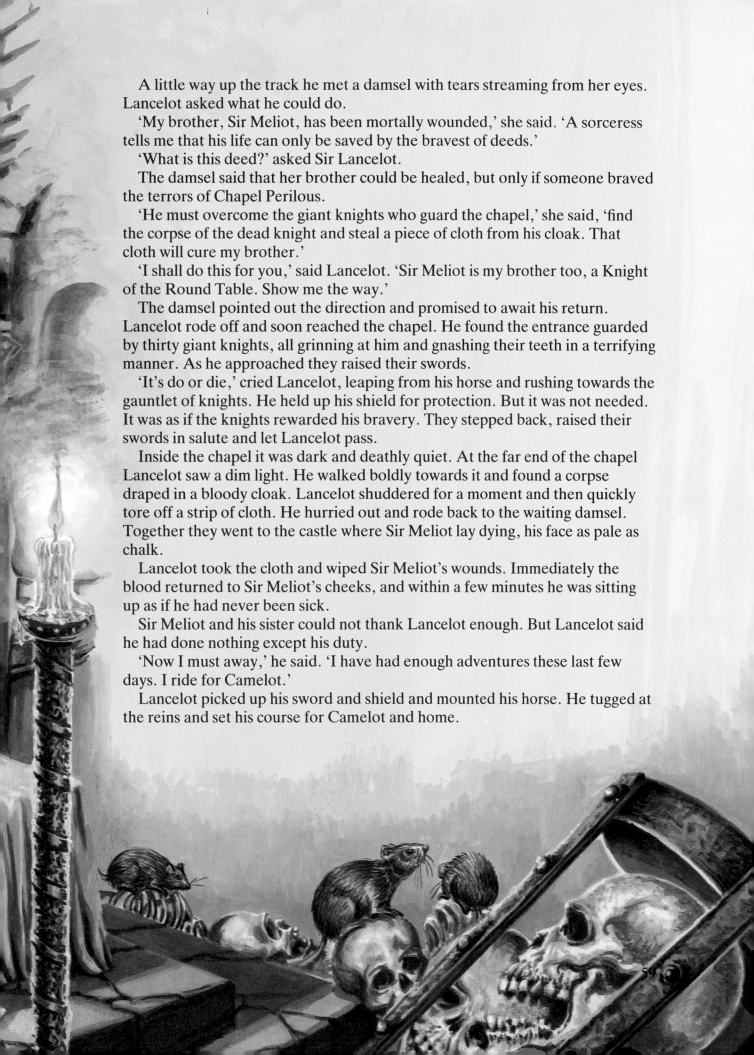

A little way up the track he met a damsel with tears streaming from her eyes. Lancelot asked what he could do.

'My brother, Sir Meliot, has been mortally wounded,' she said. 'A sorceress tells me that his life can only be saved by the bravest of deeds.'

'What is this deed?' asked Sir Lancelot.

The damsel said that her brother could be healed, but only if someone braved the terrors of Chapel Perilous.

'He must overcome the giant knights who guard the chapel,' she said, 'find the corpse of the dead knight and steal a piece of cloth from his cloak. That cloth will cure my brother.'

'I shall do this for you,' said Lancelot. 'Sir Meliot is my brother too, a Knight of the Round Table. Show me the way.'

The damsel pointed out the direction and promised to await his return. Lancelot rode off and soon reached the chapel. He found the entrance guarded by thirty giant knights, all grinning at him and gnashing their teeth in a terrifying manner. As he approached they raised their swords.

'It's do or die,' cried Lancelot, leaping from his horse and rushing towards the gauntlet of knights. He held up his shield for protection. But it was not needed. It was as if the knights rewarded his bravery. They stepped back, raised their swords in salute and let Lancelot pass.

Inside the chapel it was dark and deathly quiet. At the far end of the chapel Lancelot saw a dim light. He walked boldly towards it and found a corpse draped in a bloody cloak. Lancelot shuddered for a moment and then quickly tore off a strip of cloth. He hurried out and rode back to the waiting damsel. Together they went to the castle where Sir Meliot lay dying, his face as pale as chalk.

Lancelot took the cloth and wiped Sir Meliot's wounds. Immediately the blood returned to Sir Meliot's cheeks, and within a few minutes he was sitting up as if he had never been sick.

Sir Meliot and his sister could not thank Lancelot enough. But Lancelot said he had done nothing except his duty.

'Now I must away,' he said. 'I have had enough adventures these last few days. I ride for Camelot.'

Lancelot picked up his sword and shield and mounted his horse. He tugged at the reins and set his course for Camelot and home.

Sir Gawain and the Green Knight

Lancelot was welcomed back to Camelot as a returning hero. King Arthur and Guinevere and the Knights of the Round Table were astounded at the great feats he had achieved. Guinevere loved Lancelot more than ever.

Sir Gawain, his brother Agravain and Sir Kay, who had been rescued from the clutches of the evil Sir Turquin, went down on their knees to thank their rescuer.

Sir Meliot, whose wounds Lancelot had healed with the piece of cloth from Chapel Perilous, was in tears of gratitude.

Only Sir Gawain, the youngest warrior of the Round Table and a nephew of the king, did not think Lancelot had been completely honourable. Gawain remembered the day when Lancelot, dressed in Sir Kay's armour, had fooled him and two other knights. They had attacked Lancelot, thinking he had stolen the armour. But Lancelot had unhorsed all three and ridden off.

'Brother in arms,' King Arthur told Sir Gawain. 'Do not upset yourself. You should be proud that you were rolled over by the greatest knight of all.'

But Arthur's kind words were not enough for Gawain. He felt he had something to prove, and the brave young warrior took the first chance he had to show the Round Table that he was as worthy as any.

The opportunity came one New Year's Eve. Arthur and his warriors were feasting in the Great Hall at Camelot. But something was missing from their celebrations. They all loved to hear great stories of brave knights and enchanted castles. But, since Lancelot's return, nothing seemed to have happened.

'Life at Camelot is so quiet,' said the king. 'What would I give for some new adventures to happen.'

At that very moment the huge door to the hall crashed open and a knight on horseback rode in. The feasters were startled, looking aghast at the strange figure. He was dressed from head to foot in green. Even his horse was covered in green cloth. His face was hidden by a green helmet, yet, strangely, he wore no other armour. No knight in his right senses would ride abroad without his armour. But in his hand was a gleaming battle-axe and this he swirled above his head in the most frightening way.

'I know not who you are,' said King Arthur, 'but you are welcome to join our feast this New Year's Eve.'

The Green Knight roared his defiant answer. 'I have not come here to make merry at your feast, but to discover just how brave the Knights of the Round Table really are.'

'Knavish knight,' said the king. 'There is no challenge my gallant warriors would not accept. Come, challenge us now.'

'T'is this,' said the Green Knight. 'I am happy to allow one of your knights to take my axe and strike me with just one blow. I will not defend myself.'

'What madness is this?' said Lancelot. 'You would let us kill you with one blow and you wouldn't defend yourself?'

'That is part of the challenge,' said the Green Knight. 'The other part is that in twelve months time, on New Year's Eve, the man who strikes that blow must return to me and allow me to take one blow at him.'

'Now there,' said Arthur, 'that is a matchless challenge. Which of you is prepared to lose an arm or a leg to honour this challenge?'

The Green Knight interrupted. 'It is no arm or leg I talk about. I say who will lose a head and still think nothing of it?'

The Green Knight eyed them all, waiting to see if anyone would accept. But there was complete silence. They were thinking, firstly, that they could not kill a defenceless knight, and, secondly, that it meant certain death in a year's time if they didn't.

'What cowards you are,' cried the Green Knight. 'I knew that all I had heard about the Round Table was empty boasting.'

That was too much for King Arthur. He thundered out his reply. 'No man shall speak so of my court. I shall accept the challenge myself.'

The Green Knight was delighted. He leapt from his horse and handed Arthur his battle-axe.

The Knights of the Round Table rose as one. 'This is no challenge for our king,' they said.

'It's mine!' cried a voice from the back of the hall. It was Gawain. 'I beg you let me accept this task.'

The king and the knights tried their best to persuade Gawain to stand down. But he would not. He was set on meeting the Green Knight's terrifying test.

'Come, good knight,' said the challenger. 'Here's my axe and here's my head.'

The Green Knight knelt down and bared his neck. 'Before you strike,' he said, 'you must promise to meet me in a year's time at the Green Chapel. I shall be waiting.'

'You have my word,' said Gawain, 'but what if my blow kills you?'

'Then t'is a challenge well done, delay no more. Strike!'

Gawain raised the axe and struck the unflinching knight. The blow took off his head. Head and helmet rolled bloodily across the floor.

There was silence for a moment, and then the Green Knight's headless corpse stood up and walked towards the head. Guinevere, who was at the feast, fainted to the floor. Others cried in horror at the gruesome sight. The rest watched speechlessly as the corpse picked up its head and returned it to its shoulders.

'A good strike,' said the Green Knight. 'Now remember your promise. Meet me at the Green Chapel a year from now.'

Spring came and then Summer. The months passed too quickly for Gawain. Then it was Autumn and soon the snows of Christmas came again. Arthur felt so sorry for his young knight, but told him that he was honour-bound to meet the knight again.

New Year approached and the Knights of the Round Table held a feast to wish Gawain good luck on his terrible journey. But they all knew in their hearts that they would never see Gawain again.

Gawain had no idea where the Green Chapel was so he left Camelot several days before New Year's Eve. He too was sure that death awaited him there, but he did not want to show his fear by arriving late.

64

On Christmas Eve, the lonely knight spotted a castle. Gringalet, exhausted, gallantly carried his master to the gates. Gawain received a truly Christmas welcome from the master of the castle, Sir Bertilak. He treated him as an honoured guest and let him sit beside his beautiful young wife during the celebrations of Christmas Day.

That night Bertilak asked Gawain where he was travelling to. Gawain explained that he had to reach the Green Chapel by New Year's Eve, and asked if anyone knew where it was.

'Don't worry,' said Bertilak. 'It is close by. So relax and enjoy Christmas here. We will send you on your way in good time.'

The next day Bertilak made Gawain a strange promise. He said that he would be out hunting for the next few days. 'But I promise to give you everything I catch while I'm hunting if, in return, you give me anything which comes your way while you are in the castle.'

Gawain thanked the knight for his kindness and agreed.

The next morning after Bertilak had left for the hunt, Bertilak's wife came into Gawain's chamber and confessed that she had fallen in love with him. Gawain would not listen to her words of love. He could not dishonour the man who had given him such kind hospitality. He told her to leave and she did, but not before stealing one single kiss.

That night Bertilak returned with a deer and gave it to Gawain, who, keeping to his promise, gave the knight the only thing that had come his way that day - a kiss.

'T'is strange,' said Bertilak. 'I wonder where that kiss came from.'

The next day when Bertilak went hunting his wife came to Gawain again. Still he turned away her affections because he did not want to be disloyal. But she stole a second kiss. That night Bertilak brought Gawain a wild pig, and received the kiss in return.

On the third day Bertilak's wife came to Gawain and, despite his protestations, stole a third kiss and gave him a scarf of green silk lace to remember her by. Gawain dared not refuse her gift, but hid it beneath his cloak. When Bertilak returned that night he had a fox for the young knight. Gawain gave him the kiss but not the green silk.

'You are a lucky man,' said Bertilak. 'Each day I have been out, some pretty damsel has been giving you kisses. I would dearly love to know who gave them to you, but honour forbids me from asking you to give me her name.'

The matter was soon put aside as Gawain pointed out that the next day was New Year's Eve and asked Bertilak how he could find the Green Chapel. Bertilak explained that it was but an hour's ride away and gave him directions. That night they feasted for the last time together. Gawain shuddered at the thought of the coming day but he remained cheerful just for the sake of his kind host Sir Bertilak.

The next morning Bertilak was nowhere to be seen when Gawain got up. He saddled Gringalet and, after asking Bertilak's wife to thank her husband for his hospitality, he set off towards the Green Chapel. On the way he asked a traveller if he was on the right road.

'It is right enough,' said the man, 'but only a fool would go there. Death awaits you there.'

Gawain wished he could turn Gringalet around and escape his destiny. But bravely he continued on. Soon he entered a steep-sided gully where the track came to a dead-end in front of a high crag. Coming closer, he saw there was a narrow entrance in the rock. He dismounted and, shaking from head to foot, entered.

Gawain found himself in a dark cavern, lit only by a few candles. The flickering light cast a ghostly air. He shivered and called out in a quivering voice: 'Show yourself, Green Knight. I, Gawain, loyal knight of King Arthur, have come to honour my promise.'

'Gawain, you are as honourable man as I ever met.'

Gawain saw a figure loom from the shadows. It was the Green Knight, his battle-axe in hand.

'Whether your honour will save your head is another matter,' said the knight grimly. 'Now prepare. Let me have the blow you owe me. Kneel and bare your neck.'

Gawain knelt as the knight approached.

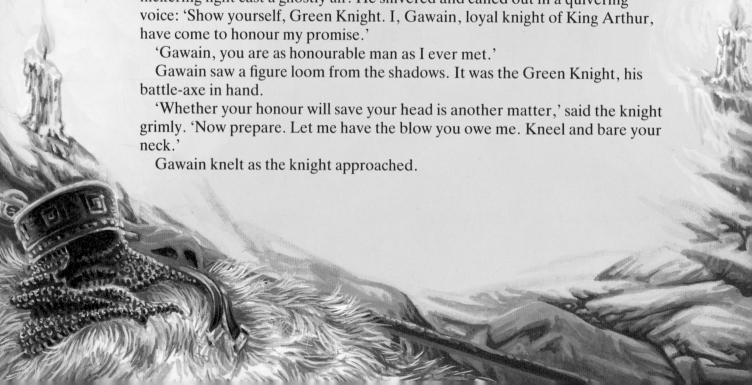

'I am ready,' said Gawain, who knew death was but a moment away.

The Green Knight raised the axe high above his head. Gawain's shoulders gave an involuntary twitch.

'Come good knight, I cannot strike while you twitch as if you were frightened,' said the axe-man.

'If I shake, it is because, unlike you sir, I cannot put back my head once it has rolled across the floor,' said Gawain.

'Come, show how brave you are,' said the Green Knight. 'Prepare again.'

Gawain hung his head and this time his courage held every muscle firm. 'Strike now!' he cried.

The Green Knight's axe fell. It sliced through the air at such a pace nothing could have stood in its path. Gawain felt it cut into the skin on the back of his neck. But nothing else.

At the last second the Green Knight had stopped the axe with a shudder. It cut a mark on Gawain's neck but nothing else. Only a few drops of blood were spilt.

Gawain slowly lifted his head and looked up. The Green Knight had taken off his helmet. Gawain recognised the face instantly. It was Bertilak.

'Good Sir Gawain,' he said. 'The challenge I gave in King Arthur's court has been well met. I could have taken your head, but there was no need. My challenge was to prove your courage and honour. You have done that. But yet I cut your neck for the fine silk my wife gave you - the one you kept a secret.'

Gawain suddenly realised Bertilak already knew where the kisses had come from. He grasped his sword, in case Bertilak struck him for those kisses.

'Have no fear,' said Bertilak. 'It was my plan. I asked my wife to tempt you with words of love. It was to test your honour and you did well. Each time she came, you turned her away. You have proved your worth in both honour and bravery. The silk scarf and the scar about your neck will be your witness that the challenge has been met.'

Bertilak took Gawain back to his castle and everyone celebrated with a huge feast. The next day Gawain left for Camelot. What a welcome he received, although some thought it must be Gawain's ghost which had returned. But Gawain showed them the scar on his neck and the green scarf. They were amazed at his story.

King Arthur embraced him warmly. 'T'is a brave knight who rides to a certain death and yet returns.'

From that day on Gawain wore the green silk scarf on his armour as a mark of true honour. Lancelot, promised his bold friend that he would never dare to play tricks on him again.

Tristram

'Shipwreck! Shipwreck!' News that a ship had been blown ashore on the coast near Camelot soon spread around the court. Lancelot and Gawain, always keen for a new adventure, galloped off to find out what they could.

They arrived to find a young knight and his servants sitting on the dunes, looking sadly at the remains of their ship. The knight, a good-looking man, was holding a beautiful harp, the only possession he had rescued from the wreck.

'Sir, t'is an unhappy day for you,' said Lancelot. 'Come, we will take you to Camelot. I am Sir Lancelot and this is Sir Gawain.'

The knight looked so unhappy, but he thanked Lancelot for his kindness and rose to his feet. 'I know of Camelot,' he said, 'and have heard of the fame of the Knights of the Round Table. Your reputation, Sir Lancelot, is known in every corner of this land. But I doubt Camelot would welcome me.'

'Nonsense,' said Gawain. 'There is always good food and a warm welcome at Camelot for any stranger. Come now. Ride with me. Your servants can follow.'

The knight reluctantly jumped up behind Sir Gawain and then asked one of his men to hand him his harp. It was evening when they reached Camelot. King Arthur and all his knights were gathered in the Great Hall, eagerly awaiting Lancelot and Gawain's return. Life had been quiet at court and they were ready to hear a good story.

It was the custom not to ask a stranger his name unless he volunteered to give it. The young knight was in no hurry to give it. Indeed, he seemed frightened in case anyone found out. But, after enjoying a fine meal, he said he would entertain them with a story about a man called the Sorrowful One.

The knight took his harp and began to play. It was the most beautiful music King Arthur and his knights had ever heard. Then, as the young man plucked sadly at the strings of his instrument, he started his story.

'It is a tale about a young man called Tristram,' said the knight. 'They called him the Sorrowful One because his mother died soon after he was born.'

The story the knight told was indeed a sad one. This is how he told it.

Soon after Tristram's mother had died, his father, King Melodias, married again. His new queen, an ambitious and plotting woman, had a son, and she was determined that he would be the next king rather than Tristram.

71

One day she put poison in a cup and carefully placed it where Tristram would see it. But the queen's own son found it first and quickly swallowed it down. He died, but no one guessed why.

The queen was horrified at what had happened, but, now, she was more determined than ever to kill Tristram. She poisoned another cup and waited for Tristram to drink it.

But King Melodias saw it first. He was about to drink it when the queen rushed in and snatched it from his hand. The king quickly realised that it had been poisoned and the queen confessed to what she had done.

The king and his council knew there was only one punishment for such a crime. The queen must be burnt to death. The fire was built and the queen, roped to an iron stake in the middle, prepared to die.

But just as the fire was about to be lit, Tristram rushed forward and begged that the queen should be given mercy. King Melodias was greatly moved by his son's request, especially as he was the queen's intended victim.

The king allowed his queen to live, but he felt it was too dangerous for Tristram to stay at court. So he was sent to France to be brought up. There he learned to speak many languages, master the arts of the sword and lance and play the harp.

When Tristram was sixteen years old he went to live with his uncle, King Mark of Cornwall at the great Castle of Tintagel. He became a strong warrior and the finest hunter anyone had ever seen. But the thing he most wanted to be was a knight.

The knight broke off from his story to take a drink.

'This is a sad story indeed,' said King Arthur, 'but a good one still.'

The king said he knew Melodias and his son Tristram. The last he had heard of the boy was when he had been sent to France. Arthur begged the knight to continue his story.

The knight began playing his harp again as he continued his story.

Tristram was eighteen years old when a messenger from King Anguish of Ireland arrived at King Mark's court. In the past the kings of Cornwall had paid tribute money to Ireland as a sign of allegiance. But it had not been paid for many years, and now King Anguish was demanding the money.

King Mark refused and the messenger was sent back to tell King Anguish that Cornwall would never pay. King Anguish was furious and sent his strongest knight, Sir Marhaus to do battle for the money. Marhaus was also a Knight of the Round Table. When he reached Cornwall, no one would fight him for the honour of Cornwall. They were frightened of fighting a Knight of the Round Table.

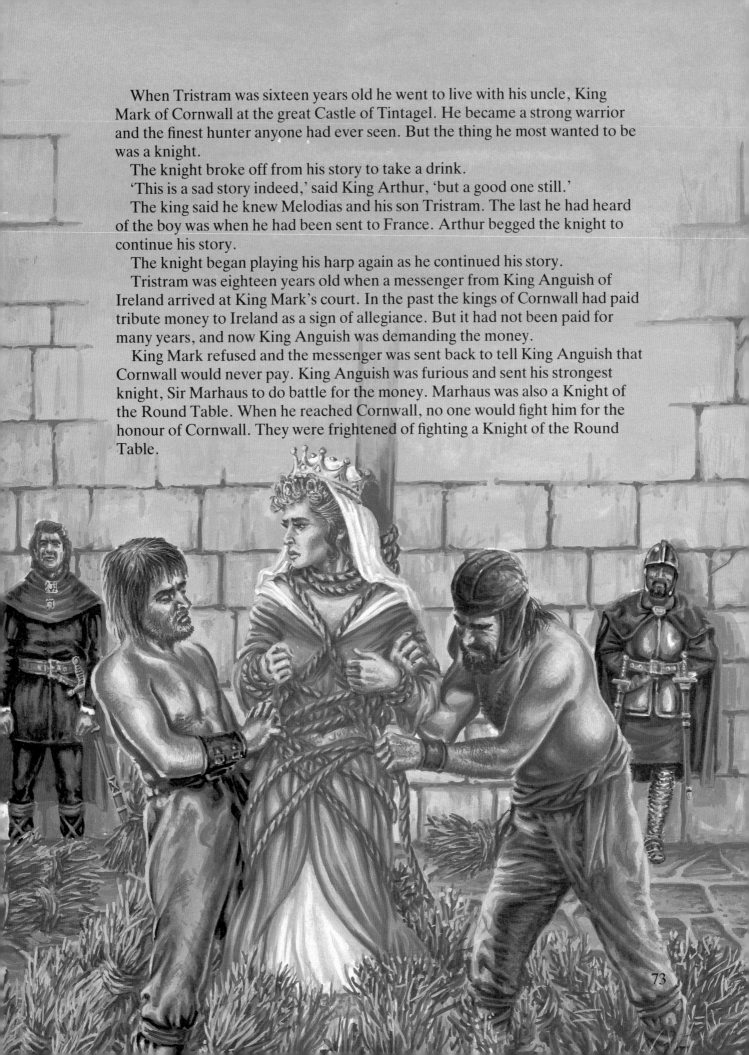

Tristram saw his chance. He stepped forward and said he would fight for Cornwall if King Mark made him a knight. The king agreed and the newly-knighted Tristram met Sir Marhaus on the field of battle.

The battle between the two lasted most of the day, but gradually the older knight tired and Tristram struck him a terrible blow on the skull. The tip of the sword pierced his head and broke off.

Mortally wounded, Sir Marhaus stumbled back to his ship and set sail for home. But he died the next day. His body was taken back to Ireland. There, his sister, the Queen of Ireland, found the tip of Tristram's sword in her brother's head. She hid it away in a chest.

Meanwhile Tristram, who had also been wounded in the battle, fell ill. It was discovered that the tip of Sir Marhaus' sword had been poisoned. Tristram was dying too.

A wise woman saw the wound and told Tristram that it could only be healed in the land where the poison had been made. Tristram knew it would be dangerous to go to Ireland. Sir Marhaus' family in Ireland would be seeking revenge for his death. But it was Tristram's only hope. So he sailed for Ireland, changing his name to Tramtrist.

Tramtrist was welcomed at the court of King Anguish and treated royally. He told the king a story that he had been wounded in a battle of honour. It happened that the king's beautiful daughter Isolde was famed for her skills with medicine. She tended Tramtrist with great love and affection and soon he was cured.

In the days which followed, Tramtrist spent many hours with Isolde. A lady of the court saw how happy they were and mixed them a love potion. The couple drank it, little knowing how powerful it was. From that moment on, Tramtrist and Isolde could not bear to be separated from each other. They became like twins and a great pain tore at their hearts if they weren't together.

The King and Queen of Ireland were happy to see their daughter in love with the young knight. But then tragedy struck. The queen chanced to see Tramtrist's sword and noticed that the tip was broken off. She hurried to her chest and took out the piece which had been taken from Sir Marhaus' head. Tramtrist's secret was out.

'Traitor,' cried the queen, holding up his sword and the broken tip. 'He is the one who killed our noble Sir Marhaus.'

The king summoned Tramtrist and told him what the queen had discovered.

'It is true,' said Tramtrist. 'My real name is Tristram. I killed Sir Marhaus in an honourable battle. I was fighting for the pride of Cornwall. Surely I have done no wrong.'

The king knew he could not be blamed. Yet he also knew it would be dangerous for the young man to stay at court. Someone might try and kill him. So the king said Tristram must return to Cornwall. Tristram was heartbroken at having to leave his beloved Isolde. She too could not have been more miserable.

'I swear,' she said to Tristram, 'that I will never marry anyone else.' Huge tears fell from her eyes as she watched Tristram sail away.

When unhappy Tristram returned home to Cornwall, he could talk of little else but his love for Isolde. Now it happened that Tristram's uncle, King Mark, had long been jealous of Tristram's good looks and bravery. The Cornish people had treated him as a hero since the battle with Sir Marhaus. King Mark schemed so cleverly. He went to Tristram one day and said: 'I have no wife. It is time I chose a queen.'

Tristram asked who he he might choose.

'There is only one,' said King Mark. 'She is of royal blood, I speak of Isolde. You must go to Ireland and bring her to me.'

Tristram's heart bled. He ached for the love of Isolde. How could he bear the thought of the king marrying her? But Tristram knew that the king must be obeyed. So sad Tristram set sail for Ireland.

Lancelot suddenly interrupted the story. 'Young knight, methinks I know the rest of this story, was not Tristram shipwrecked?'

The young knight looked up and realised that Lancelot had guessed who he was.

'Noble Sir Lancelot,' he said, 'you are as clever as you are bold. I confess it. I am Tristram. But I dared not give you my name because I killed Sir Marhaus, a Knight of the Round Table.'

The king said he had heard of the death of Sir Marhaus. 'He died in fair combat,' he said. 'You have nothing to fear in our court.'

'No,' said Sir Lancelot. 'Tristram was fighting for the honour of Cornwall.'

'And besides,' said Gawain, 'Sir Marhaus had poisoned his sword. He tried to win the battle unfairly.'

The king and his knights wanted Tristram to stay at Camelot, but he knew that he was honour-bound to continue his journey. King Arthur ordered a boat to be prepared. 'But you shall not leave,' he said, 'until we have honoured you.'

The king summoned all his knights to the Round Table and Tristram was brought in. It was Lancelot who led him to one of the seats, the one which Sir Marhaus had sat in.

'There,' said Lancelot, 'now who's name is written here?'

Tristram looked and saw that his name was inscribed on the chair. That night King Arthur made Tristram a Knight of the Round Table.

The next day Sir Tristram set sail for Ireland where he found that the queen had forgiven him for the death of her brother, and King Anguish welcomed him warmly.

'I knew you would return to claim the hand of my daughter in marriage,' he said, 'and she shall be yours.'

Tristram burst into tears. 'My Lord, I only wish I could marry her. But my uncle, King Mark, wants her for his queen.'

'Then it must be so,' said King Anguish sadly. 'A king's word, however cruel, must be obeyed. But dear Isolde will never be happy. It is a terrible thing King Mark has done.'

Isolde wept when she heard the news, but the young lovers were happy to be reunited for a while. The magic love potion never released its power and they never left each other's side as they sailed back to Cornwall. There, the unhappy bride married King Mark in the chapel at Tintagel Castle.

The days passed and the jealous king saw how Tristram and Isolde could not be kept apart. They took every chance to be together. The king was furious and ordered his cousin Sir Andred to arrest Tristram. The lovelorn knight was trussed with ropes and taken to the court house which was perched high on the cliffs. He was tried and found guilty of treason to the king.

Tristram knew the penalty was death and pleaded with his captors. 'Why are you treating me so?' he cried, 'I fought for the honour of Cornwall. Is this how I am rewarded?'

'You are traitor,' said Andred, 'and so you must die.'

Tristram was so angry he heaved at his bonds until they burst apart. He sent his guards reeling and leapt to a window ledge. He looked down to see the sea crashing on the rocks below. He had no choice. He jumped. A lucky wave broke his fall and he was washed up safely on the shore. King Mark's men raced from the court house and dashed down to the beach.

Andred saw Tristram making his escape and took out his bow. The arrow flew straight and true, piercing Tristram in the shoulder. But still Tristram ran and finally disappeared into the dusk. That night he found his way past the castle guards and reached Isolde's room. He had lost so much blood from the wound that he collapsed in her arms. When he awoke she was tending his shoulder.

'This wound is too deep,' she said. 'I cannot heal it. There is only one who can.'

Isolde told Tristram that he must sail for Brittany and seek out Isolde of the White Hands, the daughter of King Howel.

'She bears the same name as me, but she is a more powerful healer,' said Isolde.

'But when will I see you again?' said Tristram.

'I will come when I can,' she answered. 'Don't despair dearest Tristram. I shall come.'

That night Isolde's loyal servants prepared a boat and Tristram was smuggled aboard. Isolde kissed him goodbye and whispered in his ear, 'I shall come, and just so you shall know it is me, my ship will carry a white sail. If you see a ship with a black sail you shall know that I am not aboard.'

Tristram knew that every ship in those days carried black tarred sails. Few people could afford white cloth. So Tristram sailed for Brittany. King Howel welcomed Tristram and immediately sent for his daughter, Isolde of the White Hands to care for his wound.

But Tristram grew worse. Isolde of the White Hands could not cure him. She would have done anything in her power to heal Tristram because she herself had fallen in love with him. But, skilled as she was, she could not find a remedy for the wound.

Tristram knew now that only his true love could help him. Every morning he sat on the shore, playing tearful tunes on his harp, looking out to sea, desperately hoping to see a ship with white sails.

The weeks passed and Tristram grew weaker. He still sat on the shore each day but his eyes had become so weak from the poison in his body that he found it difficult to see what colour sails the boats had.

Then one morning he saw a large ship approach. He squinted and was convinced it carried white sails. His hopes rose. He cried out to Isolde of the White Hands, 'My eyes are weak, yet I am sure that ship has a white sail. Tell me you see a white sail.'

Isolde of the White Hands looked out and saw the magnificent ship approach. A beautiful lady stood on the prow and a white sail billowed above her.

Isolde of the White Hands did not speak for a moment. She loved Tristram so much that she would rather see him dead that let another have him.

'Dear Tristram,' she said, finally, 'your eyes deceive you. The sails are black.'

Tristram cried out in misery. 'My beloved Isolde will never come,' he wept. The next moment he was dead. His heart had broken for the love of Isolde.

When the ship with the white sail reached the harbour, Tristram's Isolde came ashore. It wasn't long before she found his body. Isolde embraced her dead lover and cried to the heavens. 'If we cannot share our love on Earth, then I shall meet dear Tristram in Heaven.' And with that, she died.

When King Arthur heard of the tragedy, he sent Lancelot and Gawain to bring back the bodies. They were buried together at Camelot, peaceful at last.

81

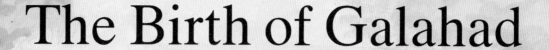

The Birth of Galahad

Sir Lancelot woke one morning at Camelot feeling the strangest sensation. He was being tugged by some invisible force, and he heard voices calling him, telling him to put on his armour and ride out.

Lancelot had no intention of riding out that day. Snow lay deep on the ground and icicles hung from the trees. There was no adventure to be had burying himself in snow. Yet, whatever force it was, it was too strong even for Lancelot. He soon found himself riding out of Camelot.

He journeyed deep into the wild forest, the snow getting deeper and deeper all the time. The forest gave way to mountains and Lancelot knew he was lost. He was so cold he wanted to stop and light a fire, but still he was led, higher and higher into the mountains.

Night fell and his horse carried him onwards and upwards. As dawn broke, he looked up through his half-frozen eyes and saw two huge castles in the distance. One stood on a high mountain peak; the other on a cliff overlooking the sea.

Soon, he clattered over a wooden bridge and came into a tiny village. He saw a group of villagers standing by a hut. They cried out when they saw him. 'Sir Lancelot! Welcome.'

Lancelot had no idea how they knew him because he was sure he had been drawn to a foreign land.

'We have waited a long time for you,' said one of the villagers. 'There is something you must do for us.'

Lancelot said he would be happy to help them, but first he wanted to know where he was.

'This is the land of Corbin,' said the villager. 'Yonder, on the mountain-top stands the Castle of Danger, the Devil's lair. And not an arrow's flight away, standing on the sea cliff, is Castle Carbonek. It is the home of King Pelles, a man of God.'

Lancelot asked what he had to do. A woman approached and said that Morgan Le Fay had been jealous of her daughter's beauty and had thrown her into the dungeon in the Castle of Danger. 'And there,' said the woman, 'they boil her every day in a cauldron.'

83

Lancelot was horrified and without hesitating, galloped up to the castle. As if by magic, the drawbridge swung down and the gates opened. Lancelot rode in and found the castle deserted. He dismounted and went down to the dungeons. He heard the damsel's despairing cries from behind a door.

Lancelot struck off the bolts with a blow from his sword. The door swung open. He was almost knocked off his feet by a blast of heat which rushed from the prison cell. Then he saw the damsel chained inside the cauldron.

It did not take Lancelot long to free her and he covered her with his cloak.

'Blessed Sir Lancelot,' she cried. 'Morgan Le Fay said that only the bravest knight of all would dare to rescue me.'

Lancelot knew that Morgan was not to be trusted, and wondered whether he had been led into a trap. He asked the damsel who was in the castle.

'Nobody, Sir Lancelot,' she answered. 'Morgan Le Fay and her evil queens left this morning - on the Devil's business no doubt.'

'Then we must be gone before she returns,' said Lancelot. They hurried up into the daylight again. Lancelot, with the damsel sitting behind him, rode out of the castle. Lancelot noticed a large tombstone by the castle gate and stopped to read its inscription.

84

"A LEOPARD OF KING'S BLOOD WILL SLAY THE DRAGON INSIDE THIS TOMB. AND THEN HE WILL FATHER A LION AMONG MEN, A KNIGHT WHO WILL BECOME THE MOST CHRISTIAN IN THE LAND".

'What can this mean?' asked Lancelot.

'King Ban was your father, therefore you are of a king's blood,' said the damsel, 'so it is doubtless that you are the Leopard. The Lion is the son you shall have one day.'

Lancelot was puzzled by what she said. How did she know so much about him? He could feel enchantment in the air. He got off his horse and heaved at the great stone covering the tomb. He had only moved it a few inches when a dragon, spitting fire and brimstone, burst out.

It spat a column of fire at Lancelot. But he managed to protect himself from the fiery attack with his shield. Then he leapt onto its long neck, his sword at the ready. With one blow, he took off the monster's head.

'The first part of this magic is finished,' said the damsel. 'You have proved that you are the one King Pelles is waiting for.'

85

Lancelot heard her words but, when he turned around, the damsel was nowhere to be seen. The cloak he had lent the damsel now lay on the ground. Just then an old lady appeared from behind the tomb.

'Stand where you are,' cried Lancelot, raising his sword. 'Don't try your magic on me.'

'You have nothing to fear from me,' said the woman. 'They call me Dame Brisen, an enchantress indeed, but for good, not evil. Come with me.'

Lancelot was powerless to resist. He followed Dame Brisen all the way from the Castle of Danger to Castle Carbonek. King Pelles was waiting for him.

The king, a kindly and friendly-faced man, gave Lancelot a warm welcome and invited him to share a feast that night. Elaine, the king's beautiful daughter, joined them at the table. Lancelot had never tasted such good food, or drunk such fine wine.

Later that night Dame Brisen took Lancelot and showed where he could sleep. So many strange things had happened that day that Lancelot wanted to stay awake and watch out for danger. But Dame Brisen had made sure he wouldn't with a potion mixed into the wine. Lancelot immediately fell into a deep sleep.

He awoke the next morning to see Elaine, the king's daughter, in his room. She spoke to him in a loving voice. 'We have been brought together by magic to fulfill a great prophecy. In time I will give birth to your son, and he shall be called Galahad. He will sit beside you at the Round Table.'

Lancelot was astonished at her words. He could not understand what had happened during the night. 'This place is enchanted. I will have no more of it.'

Lancelot raced from the room, found his horse and galloped away. He crossed the bridge in the village and took the road for Camelot. No more snow had fallen during that magical night and he quickly retraced his own snowprints. Lancelot reached Camelot in no time at all.

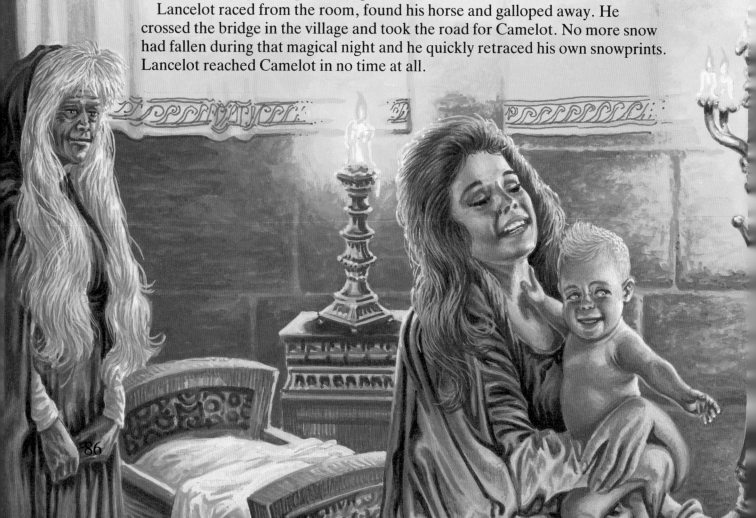

Months passed and in time the baby Galahad was born to Elaine. The enchantress Dame Brisen said that someone must take the news to Camelot. Dame Brisen quickly went to work. Lancelot's nephew, Sir Bors, was riding close by Castle Carbonek and he was soon enticed to the castle gate. He was taken to see the child.

'T'is strange,' said Sir Bors, 'but he has Lancelot's eyes.'

'It is true,' said Elaine. 'Galahad is our child. Nacien the holy hermit prophecied that it should happen.'

An old man entered the room at that moment. It was Nacien. He looked as old as the hills and shuffled over to speak to Sir Bors. 'Elaine speaks the truth,' he said. 'Mark you well, Sir Bors, this child will take his place at King Arthur's Round Table.'

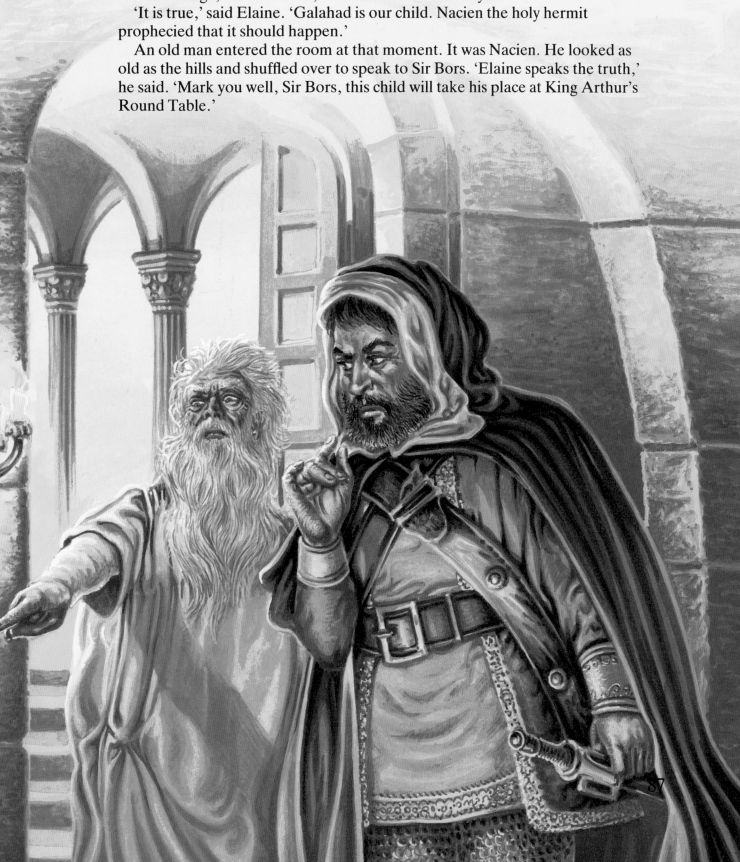

'And where shall he sit?' asked Sir Bors, 'there is but one place left, and that is the Siege Perilous. Merlin said only the most Christian knight could take that place.'

'Sir Galahad will rightly claim that seat when he is fifteen years old,' said Nacien, 'but for now he will be taken from here and brought up in a nunnery. I will bring him to Camelot when the time is right.'

That night Nacien appeared in a dream to Sir Bors and told him the story of Joseph of Arimathea, the disciple who took Jesus' body from the cross and laid it in a tomb.

'Remember,' echoed Nacien's voice, 'remember how Joseph brought Christianity to this land; and how he brought with him the Holy Grail, the cup which Jesus drank from at the Last Supper. Is that not the cup which every knight would dearly love to drink from?'

Sir Bors heard his own voice answering. 'If we could, we would die happy men.'

Nacien continued: 'Few of King Arthur's knights will ever see it, let alone drink from it. But Galahad will show all the other knights what a true Christian is. He will find the Holy Grail.'

When Sir Bors awoke, he did not know what to make of all he had seen and heard in his dreams. He hurried back to Camelot and told the court what happened.

When Queen Guinevere heard about the birth of Galahad she was furious. She summoned Lancelot.

'Oh, faithless knight,' she said. 'Have I not loved you dearly since you came to this court? Have you not always worn my colours in battle? How could you love another? You shall be banished from Camelot forever!'

Lancelot was horrified. He pleaded with the queen, trying to explain how he had been enchanted by powerful magic. 'I was powerless to do anything.'

But the queen had made up her mind. 'Be gone,' she said.

It was too much for Lancelot who had loved Guinevere since he first set eyes on her. He had remained faithful to both the queen and King Arthur for many years and now he was being banished because of Dame Brisen's wily magic. The shame was too much for him. He let out the cry of a madman, shrieking and groaning in a terrible manner. He threw off his armour and, dressed only in a shirt and breeches, leapt out of the window. Shouting wildly, and completely out of his wits, he ran off into the forest.

The Search for Lancelot

Lancelot disappeared into the forest, ranting and raving like a madman. Wearing just a shirt and breeches, he rampaged through the woods whirling his sword in the air and attacking anyone who crossed his path. An unlucky dwarf met him in a glade and Lancelot bundled him cruelly to the ground. 'What has happened to our noble Sir Lancelot?' said the dwarf, holding his painful head.

For months on end Lancelot continued on his journey of mayhem. Soon he became almost unrecognisable. His clothes were caked with dirt and he was as thin as a skeleton. Wild berries from the hedgerows were all he ate. Now and again travellers spotted the sad figure roaming alone. They brought the news to Camelot.

King Arthur was puzzled why Lancelot had suddenly gone out of his mind, but Queen Guinevere was very distressed because she had found out that Lancelot had been under the power of magic when he met Elaine.

'Lancelot must be found,' she said, 'and brought back to Camelot. He must be told that he is still our most dear and noble knight.'

Guinevere said she would pay whatever it cost to bring him back and asked the Knights of the Round Table to begin the search. Lancelot's brother, Sir Ector de Maris was the first to volunteer. He was joined by Lancelot's cousin Sir Bors.

They set off and searched high and low for Lancelot, riding through England, Scotland and Wales. But they neither saw nor heard anything of the unhappy knight.

Many months later Lancelot reached the enchanted lands of Corbin. He had no idea that he had been there before. He could not remember freeing the damsel from the cauldron, killing the dragon or meeting with King Pelles and Elaine. He was in such a state that no one remembered him either. As he ran through the streets, youths jeered and laughed at him. Lancelot broke a few of their arms and legs before he was captured by some men belonging to Castor, the nephew of King Pelles of Castle Carbonek.

Castor, not knowing who he was, appointed him court jester. What a sad joker Lancelot made. The proudest knight in the world was now just a figure of fun.

One day Castor took him to King Pelles' castle. Even the king didn't recognise Lancelot. Yet he knew that the man must have been a knight at some time because of all the battle scars on his body.

The stranger in the castle caused a lot of interest. Everyone wondered who he was. In the afternoon Lancelot fell asleep in the castle gardens. Elaine happened to be walking there and could not resist taking a closer glance. Love saw through Lancelot's madness. Elaine's eyes opened wide in amazement.

'Could it be?' she murmured, looking even closer into the stranger's eyes. 'Lancelot! It is my dearest Lancelot. He has come back to me.'

Elaine ran off to find Dame Brisen, excitedly shouting that Lancelot had returned.

Dame Brisen had already guessed who the stranger was, and knew that she was the only one with enough magic to cure him. She hurried with Elaine to Lancelot's side.

'I am the one who caused all his misery,' she said. 'I was the one who had to enchant him so that Galahad could be born. I caused the unhappiness between Lancelot and Guinevere. So now I must cure him of his madness.'

She put her hands over his sleeping eyes and summoned the spirits of good to enter his body. Elaine watched closely and saw the misery on Lancelot's face slowly fade. Years of pain and anguish fell away. Then he awoke.

'Where am I?' he asked. 'Elaine! What am I doing here?'

Elaine answered him gently. 'You are cured now, but you arrived here as a madman. You were out of your wits with grief and trouble. Dame Brisen has healed you.'

Lancelot was horrified when he heard what had happened to him. 'I can never return to Camelot,' he said. 'I would be too ashamed to show myself.'

93

Lancelot asked King Pelles to let him live in one of his castles. 'I shall change my name,' said Lancelot, 'so nobody will know who I am. From now on I shall be known as The Wandering Knight.'

So Lancelot and Elaine went to live at Castle Bliant, an island fortress surrounded by deep water. Elaine loved Lancelot so dearly, but Lancelot still yearned to see Guinevere, King Arthur and Camelot again. Every day he stood on the castle battlements and looked sadly towards the land of Camelot.

Lancelot's brother Sir Ector de Maris and Sir Bors had hunted high and low to find Lancelot without success. They had almost given up and were on their way home to Camelot when they passed Castle Bliant.

Sir Ector looked across the water to the castle and bellowed out: 'Who lives in this place?'

A voice echoed back, 'The most courageous and brave knight in the world. He calls himself The Wandering Knight.'

'Then he is a boaster,' roared Sir Ector. 'My brother Lancelot is the bravest knight of all.'

Elaine heard the reply and knew she could not keep Lancelot from his brother. She sent a boat to bring the visitors to the castle. She told them all about Lancelot's adventures and how he was too ashamed to return home.

When Lancelot saw his brother he fell into his arms and wept. 'Dear brother, it is good to see you again. And welcome Sir Bors.' Sir Ector begged Lancelot to return with them to Camelot.

'The king and the queen miss you so much,' he said. 'Queen Guinevere herself has paid twenty thousand pounds in silver for the Knights of the Round Table to find you. If you return with us, there will never be a knight who is more welcome at Camelot.'

Lancelot was moved by his brother's words and knew he must return. Elaine burst into tears. Once more she was to lose the man she loved.

'I will die for the love of you,' she said. 'But Galahad will keep me in your memory. And you will see him soon.'

Lancelot rode away with the two Knights of the Round Table. Elaine stood on the battlements and watched them go. Tears flooded down her face as Lancelot disappeared into the distance.

But there was great joy in the court at Camelot when Lancelot returned. Queen Guinevere wept with happiness and King Arthur was delighted to see his favourite knight home again.

95

Galahad Comes to Camelot

Spring blossom filled the hedgerows as the Knights of the Round Table gathered at Camelot to celebrate the feast of Pentecost on Whitsunday. Two days before the celebration a damsel arrived with a message from King Pelles of Castle Carbonek.

'The king says that Sir Lancelot must come with me tonight,' she said.

Guinevere was worried. 'But that means he will miss the feast.'

But the damsel was insistent, and promised that Lancelot would be back in time.

Lancelot asked what King Pelles wanted but the damsel would not tell him. 'You will find out when you reach your destination.'

Lancelot left with the damsel. They rode through the forest for a day and a night before reaching the land of Corbin once more. The damsel took Lancelot to an abbey near Castle Carbonek and told him to enter alone.

Inside he saw twelve nuns sitting with a youth of about fifteen years of age. Lancelot stared into the young man's eyes.

'Galahad?' he whispered. 'Are you my son, Galahad?'

One of the nuns answered him. 'This is your son. We have brought him up these last fifteen years. Soon he will take his place at King Arthur's Round Table.'

Lancelot walked slowly across and held out his arms. Galahad looked at his father for a moment, seeing the battle-weary eyes, the scars and the pain he had suffered over the years. Then they embraced.

Lancelot wanted to take his son back to Camelot that night, but Galahad said the time had not yet come.

'Ride home, Father,' he said, 'I will be with you soon. And you will speed my journey if you knight me now.'

Lancelot saw what a handsome and well-built man his son had become and, without hesitating, told him to kneel. The blade of Lancelot's sword touched both shoulders.

'Arise, Sir Galahad,' said the proud father.

Lancelot reached Camelot as the dawn was coming up. He said nothing about what he had seen and joined the other knights at the Round Table.
Lancelot saw that every seat at the table was taken except for the Siege Perilous.

'Remember Merlin,' said King Arthur. 'Remember how he said that no man should use that seat until the coming of the most Christian knight of all.'

'I think that time is not far off,' said Lancelot. Just then a traveller entered.

'I have seen the strangest sight,' he said. 'A stone floating in the river. And there is a sword sticking from it.'

Everyone hurried down to the river and saw that it was true. Floating by the river bank was a huge stone with a magnificent sword protruding from it. Gawain waded in and took a closer look.

'It has an inscription on the hilt,' he shouted back to the others. 'It says: "This sword shall hang at the side of the most Christian knight of all."'

Gawain tried to pull the sword from the stone but it would not move. The king told Lancelot to try his hand. But he did not want to try.

'This sword is not for me, yet I think I know whose it is.'

'This is a great marvel,' said the king. 'Let us go and eat. Perhaps this mystery will be revealed to us later.'

The knights returned to the castle and sat down to eat. There was an air of excitement and anticipation at the Round Table that night. And no one was to be disappointed. Suddenly the doors to the Great Hall slammed shut without a man laying a hand on them. Then the window shutters locked themselves. The Knights of the Round Table looked around, wondering what was going on.

Then, in the dim light, a figure appeared by the door. It was the old hermit, Nacien. He was dressed in white, and behind him was a young knight clothed in red.

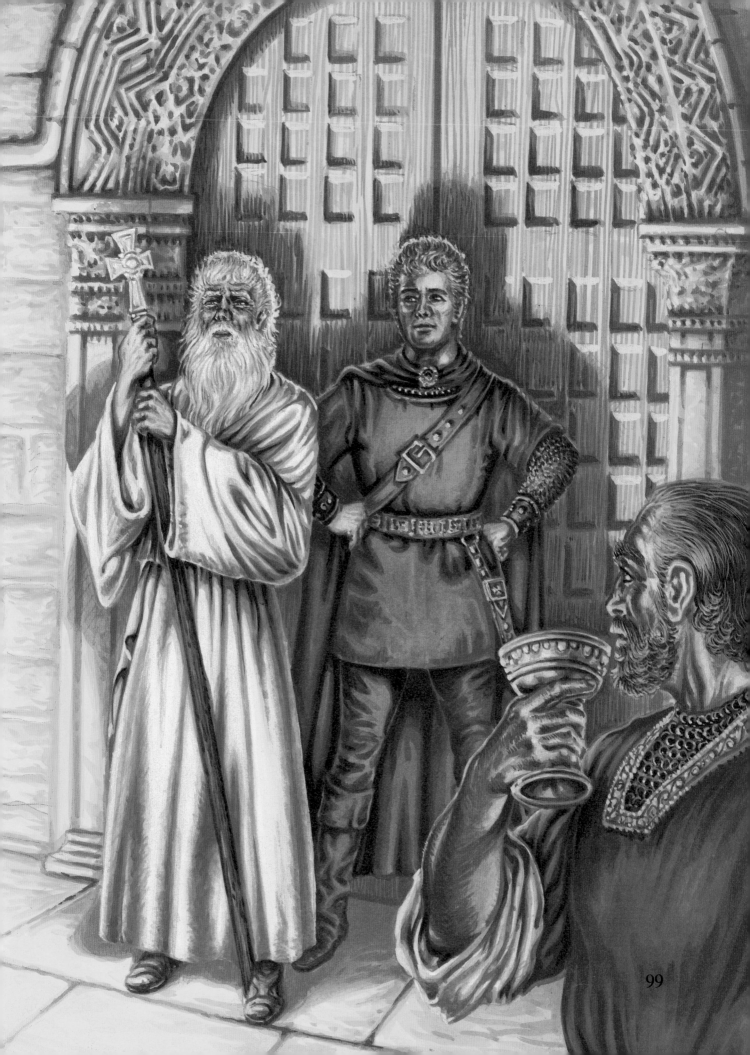

99

As their eyes became accustomed to the light, they saw the old man lead the young man to the empty chair, the Siege Perilous. He lifted the cloth of silk which covered the seat and King Arthur and his knights were amazed to see that the chair now bore an inscription in bright gold letters.

"THIS IS THE SEAT OF SIR GALAHAD".

The young knight took his seat at the Round Table.

Lancelot was the first to speak. 'Galahad, you are most welcome at our table.'

'Welcome, Sir Galahad,' said King Arthur, quickly spotting the likeness between the young knight and Lancelot. 'We have waited long for your arrival. It was long ago when Merlin prophesied your coming.'

Arthur noticed that Sir Galahad had neither sword nor shield. The scabbard at his side was empty.

'Sir Galahad,' he said. 'We are all mystified at a sword we saw this morning.'

'That is no mystery,' said Galahad, 'as you shall see.'

Once more everyone went down to the river and Galahad waded to the floating stone. He grasped the sword and pulled it out without any effort at all. He slipped it into his empty scabbard. It fitted perfectly.

100

On their way back to the castle, Guinevere spied the young knight and knew immediately that it was Lancelot's son.

'You are welcome,' she said. 'You will doubtless prove a match for your gallant and noble father.'

That night they celebrated the feast of Pentecost at the Round Table. It was the first time that all one hundred and fifty seats at the table were occupied. King Arthur looked proudly on the scene.

Suddenly there was a great clap of thunder which shook the Castle of Camelot to its foundations. Lightning lit up the sky, and then a strange darkness filled the room.

A beam of light appeared from nowhere. It was so bright the knights covered their eyes for a moment. When they looked again, they saw a silk cloth dancing in the beam.

Looking closer, they saw that the cloth was hiding something. They saw a faint shadow; it was the shape of a cup. Every knight gasped. They knew that the cloth must be hiding the Holy Grail, the vessel which Jesus had drunk from at the Last Supper before his crucifixion. But they could not see it properly, and, the harder they looked, the dimmer it became. Finally the beam, the cloth and the shadow behind it drifted high into the ceiling and vanished.

King Arthur went down on his knees and praised God. His knights did the same. But no one spoke for a while. The appearance of the Holy Grail had stunned everyone.

Gawain was the first to speak.

'It is a sign from Joseph of Arimathea who brought this holy vessel to England hundreds of years ago. It is a sign that God is angry with us. He is taking the cup away from us.'

Many of the knights asked what they should do now.

'We must show God that we will mend our ways,' said Gawain. 'Today we saw its shadow, but only those who see it clearly will have God's grace. We must go in search of the Holy Grail.'

Everyone in the room, except King Arthur, agreed.

'Beware of Merlin's prophesy,' he said. 'He warned that one day the fellowship of the Knights of the Round Table would be destroyed. This could be the time.'

Lancelot interrupted. 'But my Lord, this quest will bring us great glory.'

'That is what concerns me,' said the king. 'My knights seek honour for themselves, rather than for God. The Holy Grail will not be seen by anyone who values their own honour more than God's.'

But the knights would not be persuaded and the next morning all one hundred and fifty Knights of the Round Table gathered at the castle gate to set off on their quest.

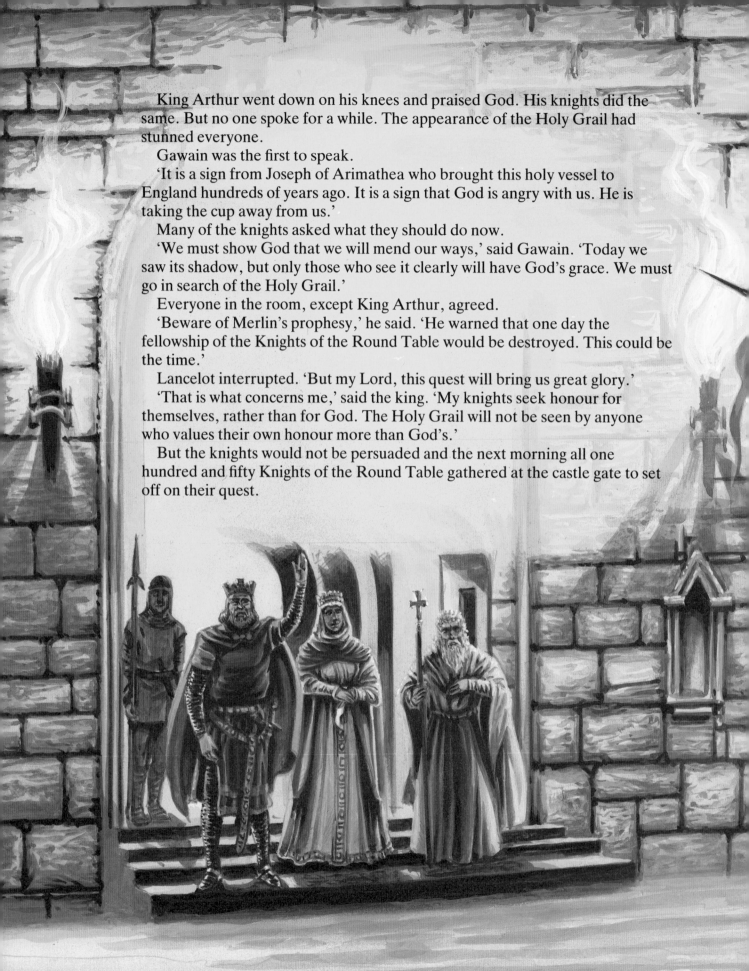

There were tears in King Arthur's eyes. 'My love goes with you on this quest, but I wish it wasn't so. Many of you will not return. Some of you will lose your lives. This is the last time we will all be together.'

It was the saddest day that Camelot had ever seen. King Arthur's last words were to Lancelot.

'Dear, Sir Lancelot. I have loved you as my most loyal and noble knight. I bid you farewell, but you leave me with a great sadness in my heart.'

But even then Sir Lancelot was thinking about the glory of the quest for the Holy Grail. He raised his lance in salute and galloped away.

103

The Quest for the Holy Grail

The streets of Camelot echoed to the sound of six hundred hooves as the one hundred and fifty Knights of the Round Table set out in search of the Holy Grail.

Each knight wished the others good luck on their journey and rode off in all directions. Some travelled north, some south, others east and west. All hoped that God would lead them to the Holy Grail and all yearned for the glory of finding it.

Sir Galahad, with his new-found sword but still without a shield, rode on alone. On the evening of the fourth day he reached an abbey. He found that two other Knights of the Round Table were already there.

Sir Bagdemagus was most excited. 'We have found a wonderful secret here,' he said. 'In this abbey there is a huge, heavy shield. It is said that only the rightful owner can bear it safely. All others will suffer injury or even death if they dare to try it. But glory I seek, and so tomorrow I shall try my luck.'

The next day a monk took them to the altar in the abbey and showed them the shield. It had a red cross on it.

'I will try it,' said Bagdemagus.

'Be warned,' said the monk. 'It could bring your death.'

But Bagdemagus insisted. He took the shield and mounted his horse. 'Death or glory,' he shouted.

He hadn't gone far when a knight, dressed completely in white, appeared on a hill above him. Bagdemagus saluted him with the shield. It was as if he had waved a red rag at a bull.

The White Knight charged down on him at a furious pace. Bagdemagus hardly had time to raise his lance before the mysterious knight was on him. The knight clouted Bagdemagus across the head with his shield, knocking him to the ground senseless.

When Bagdemagus recovered, the White Knight was standing above him. 'That shield does not belong to you,' said the knight. 'I could have killed you for carrying it. The shield belongs to the most Christian knight of all, Sir Galahad. Take it to him.'

Bagdemagus, still shaking from his encounter, galloped back to the abbey as quickly as he could and found Galahad. He explained what had happened and gave him the shield.

Young Galahad immediately rode out with the shield to find the White Knight. He wanted to know why it belonged to him. Soon after the White Knight galloped up to him.

'Sir, tell me the history of this shield,' said Galahad.

The White Knight told him that Joseph of Arimathea had brought the shield to England with the Holy Grail. On his death bed, he had painted the red cross with his own blood, vowing that no man should carry the shield until the coming of Galahad.

'Why me?' asked Galahad.

'You are related to Joseph by blood. Your blood is linked across the centuries to his. He ordered that the shield be kept at the abbey near here until your arrival.'

Galahad was amazed at the story. He thanked the White Knight who rode away in an unearthly silence and vanished into the mists.

Lancelot rode for several weeks without finding any clue to the whereabouts of the Holy Grail. One evening he reached a stone cross which marked the spot where three roads went different ways. He saw a ghostly light hovering around a chapel close by. He tied his horse to a tree, took off his sword and shield and laid them on the ground. Then he went to investigate.

The chapel windows were glowing brightly from a strange light inside. Lancelot was sure he had reached the end of his quest. He was sure the Holy Grail was inside. He tried to open the door, but it was locked and bolted. He tried the windows, but they were locked too. He sat down to think and soon felt terribly tired. He fell asleep. When he awoke he saw to his dismay that someone had stolen his horse, sword and armour. Lancelot cried out in misery. 'Oh, unhappy knight. I am not allowed to see the Holy Grail and now my horse has been stolen.'

Lancelot got up and walked away sadly from the chapel. After a while he came to a lonely hermitage, and there he found Nacien.

'Good sir, I seek help,' said Lancelot. 'I have lost everything. God has deserted me. Even my horse has been stolen. I curse my very birth.'

Nacien looked at Lancelot and told him to unburden his worries.

Lancelot told Nacien everything. He confessed to his love for Guinevere and to how he had cruelly left Elaine before Galahad was born; and how he had only fought his battles to win the queen's honour, rather than God's.

When Lancelot had finished, Nacien spoke. 'Sir Lancelot you have much to thank God for. He has given you courage, good looks and riches. But you used these for your own glory. You used these gifts to find fame and fortune for yourself, and to make Guinevere love you. You should have used them for God's purpose.'

Lancelot vowed there and then to change his ways. As Lancelot walked away into the night, he heard Nacien call after him, 'Your horse and armour aren't far away. When you have found them, ride for the coast. You must meet someone there.'

Lancelot was delighted to find that his horse and weapons had been returned to where he had left them, and the next day he galloped off towards the coast. It was nightfall when he reached a lonely and rocky shore, a place where no ship could berth. But, to his surprise, he saw a ship moored against the rocks. He dismounted and clambered down.

The ship had neither oars nor sail. It was draped in black silk. Once aboard, he realised that the ship was empty. He settled down to sleep. He had just closed his eyes when he heard the thunder of approaching hooves. He looked out into the darkness and saw a horseman pulling up at the side of the ship.

'Father!' The voice was well-known to Lancelot.

'My son. My dear Galahad!' replied Lancelot.

Galahad came aboard and they hugged each other.

'What brings you here?' asked Lancelot.

'I had a dream. Nacien the Hermit told me to come.'

Suddenly they heard someone else arrive outside the ship. It was the mysterious White Knight who had spoken to Galahad about his shield.

'I have brought you here to say farewell to each other,' he said in a kind and gentle voice. 'Sir Galahad must continue on his quest for the Holy Grail. You will not meet again on this Earth, but, Lancelot, I promise you that your own quest for the Holy Grail is not completely lost.'

So Lancelot blessed his son and the tears fell as they embraced each other for the last time.

Galahad mounted his horse and rode off into the darkness with the White Knight. Lancelot was left alone on the ship. Soon he was asleep. When he awoke he saw that the ship had drifted far out to sea.

It drifted all that day, but as night fell it reached the shore again. Lancelot made out the vague shape of a castle perched above him on the clifftops. It was Castle Carbonek. He climbed the cliffs and found his way to a rear gate.

Lancelot walked in and felt drawn to one of the upstairs rooms. The door was locked, but he could hear unearthly voices, singing sweetly from behind it. He knew he had found the Holy Grail once more. He knelt down and prayed. 'If ever in my life I did one good thing, please show me something of the Holy Grail.'

Miraculously the door opened. A brilliant light burst out and a voice warned him not to enter the room. Lancelot looked up and saw that in the middle of the room was a silver table. Standing on it, but hidden beneath a cloth of red silk, was the Holy Grail. The temptation was too much. Lancelot stepped into the room.

A fierce blast of hot air struck him in the face. It sent him tumbling to the floor. That was the last thing he knew for a long time. He regained consciousness three weeks later. He found himself in bed. Dame Brisen was nursing him.

'Where am I?' he asked.

'You are in Castle Carbonek,' said Dame Brisen. 'We all thought you were dead when we found you.'

King Pelles visited him that day and brought sad news. 'My daughter Elaine has died,' he said. 'She passed away soon after you left her last.'

Lancelot wept. 'I treated her cruelly.'

'It is for that reason,' said the king, 'that you were not allowed to see the Holy Grail itself.'

Lancelot held King Pelles' hands and begged to be forgiven. 'I am just eternally grateful that I have been allowed to come so close to it. It's all I deserve.'

That night Lancelot's brother, Sir Ector de Maris, reached Castle Carbonek. He, like many of the Knights of the Round Table, had given up all hope of finding the Holy Grail. He was delighted to find Lancelot in the castle and persuaded him to join him on the journey home.

So, a year after leaving on the quest, Lancelot and Sir Ector de Maris reached Camelot again. King Arthur rode out to greet them. 'Thank God you are safely returned,' said the king. Guinevere burst into tears of joy when she heard that Lancelot was back.

That evening, the knights met again at the Round Table. As King Arthur had foretold, many had not returned. Some had been killed by the king's enemies. Some had got lost in the wild forests and died of hunger. Others had been enchanted away by evil sorcerers. King Arthur had lost nearly half of his one hundred and fifty knights.

But Sir Gawain and his brothers Gaheris, Agravain and Gareth had returned. So too had Arthur's ambitious nephew, Sir Mordred.

The king asked if anyone had any news of Sir Bors or Sir Galahad. Lancelot told of his meeting with Galahad, but no one had seen him, or Sir Bors, recently.

'Without doubt,' said the king, 'those two are the holiest knights. Their hearts belong to God first and their king second. God will look after them.'

Even as they spoke, Sir Galahad and Sir Bors were still on their travels in search of the Holy Grail … each alone, yet destined to meet.

The Ghost of Joseph of Arimathea

There was a stone cross close to Castle Carbonek which marked the place where three lonely forest tracks joined. It was there that King Arthur's two holiest knights met.

Sir Galahad and Sir Bors emerged from the dark forest at the same time. They could not believe their eyes. One moment they had been riding their long and lonely track; the next they were together.

'God bless you brother,' said Sir Bors. 'I have not met anyone for months. All I have seen is wild forests, deserted valleys and chilly mountain tops.'

The two spent a while telling each other about their adventures, and then Galahad said they should find a place to sleep that night. 'We are near Castle Carbonek. King Pelles will give us shelter.'

They rode on until they reached the castle. King Pelles was so pleased to see them arrive safely. 'Nacien the Hermit said that you two would reach this castle together.'

King Pelles led the two knights to an upstairs chamber and left them alone, closing the door behind him.

The knights shivered. The room was dark, silent and cold. But then a light appeared in a corner. It grew brighter and brighter, and the room became warmer. Then they saw a shadowy figure. It was an old man, so ancient and thin. He was carrying a silver cross in one hand and the Holy Grail itself in the other.

'Don't be afraid,' said the old man. 'I am Joseph of Arimathea who first brought Christianity to England. I am a ghost now, but I was of this earth once. That was many hundreds of years ago.'

The knights knelt in silence as he spoke.

'Evil has come to this country and the Grail must now return to the Holy Land from where I brought it. You will take it back for me. A ship will be ready for you in the morning.'

113

They were the last words they heard. The figure disappeared, taking the Holy Grail with him. The next morning Galahad and Bors found the ship. In the middle of the deck stood the Holy Grail, covered in red silk.

The magical ship carried them out to sea, and soon both knights were deeply asleep. Who knows how long they slept, but when they awoke, they found themselves berthed in the harbour of the holy city of Sarras.

Galahad carried the Holy Grail as they left the ship and walked towards the city. They met a crippled man at the gate and Galahad asked him to help him carry the Grail.

'I cannot, stranger,' said the cripple. 'I have not walked for ten years.'

'Then rise to your feet now - and you will,' said Galahad.

The man rose slowly to his feet and found that he had been cured. 'It is a miracle!' he cried.

When the heathen king of the city heard what had happened he became frightened of the strangers' powers. He sent soldiers to arrest them. Sir Galahad and Sir Bors were put into a dungeon. The Holy Grail was thrown in with them.

But after a year the king fell ill. He knew he was going to die and sent for the knights. He asked for their forgiveness. Galahad blessed him and the king died a Christian.

The wise men of the city decided that only one man could succeed the king. Galahad was chosen and crowned.

He ruled the city for a year and then, on Easter Day, he summoned Sir Bors. 'This will be our last time together,' he said. 'We must share a final Easter feast.'

They drank together from the Holy Grail and, when they had finished, Sir Galahad lifted his hands to Heaven and called out: 'Lord, I thank you. My earthly quest is over.'

The figure of Joseph of Arimathea appeared as Galahad embraced his friend. His final words were to Sir Bors. 'Send my blessing to my dear father, Sir Lancelot.'

Sir Bors watched as Joseph of Arimathea took Sir Galahad by the hand and led him a little distance away. Then he saw a vision of Galahad's soul ascending into heaven, the Holy Grail disappearing with him.

After Sir Galahad died, Sir Bors sailed home to England and reached Camelot once more. The Knights of the Round Table who had survived the quest marvelled at his story. But none more so than Sir Lancelot. He wept when he heard how Galahad had sent him special blessings.

'We had but a little while together,' said Lancelot. 'But he was surely the most Christian knight of all.'

115

Mordred's Plot

Sir Mordred, the king's nephew, had been doing all he could to cause trouble at the court of Camelot. His burning ambition had always been to steal King Arthur's throne. His hatred for Lancelot burned as strongly.

Few people liked the scheming Mordred. His only ally was Agravain, Gawain's brother. He took Mordred's side because he had long been envious of all the praise and glory heaped on Lancelot.

The court at Camelot had been gossiping for a long time about Lancelot's love for the queen. But it was always kept secret from the king. Many thought he knew.

But one day Mordred and Agravain announced that they were going to tell King Arthur about it. The other knights saw how it was just another of Mordred's evil schemes. Gawain glared at the two men.

'Lancelot loves both the king and the queen,' he said, 'and he has served them both better than any knight in this kingdom. That's more than can be said of you two dishonourable scoundrels. And you Agravain my brother, you owe Lancelot your life. But for him, you would still be rotting in Turquin's dungeon.'

But Mordred and Agravain went to King Arthur one night and told him all. 'We are both sons of your sisters,' said Mordred, 'and we cannot bear the dishonour being done to you by Sir Lancelot. He is a traitor!'

King Arthur put his head in his hands. He had always been a wise king, and had long known of Lancelot's love for Guinevere. Merlin had warned him it would happen. But Arthur loved both Guinevere and Lancelot equally, and he knew that his favourite knight was not a traitor.

'Mordred and Agravain,' said the king. 'You are mischief-makers bent on making trouble.'

'We shall prove we are not,' said Mordred.

That night Mordred and Agravain sent a servant girl to Lancelot to tell him that the queen wished to see him urgently. Lancelot hurried to Guinevere's chamber. No sooner had he entered than the two conspirators, helped by twelve discontented knights, arrived outside.

'Come out, traitor,' shouted Mordred.

116

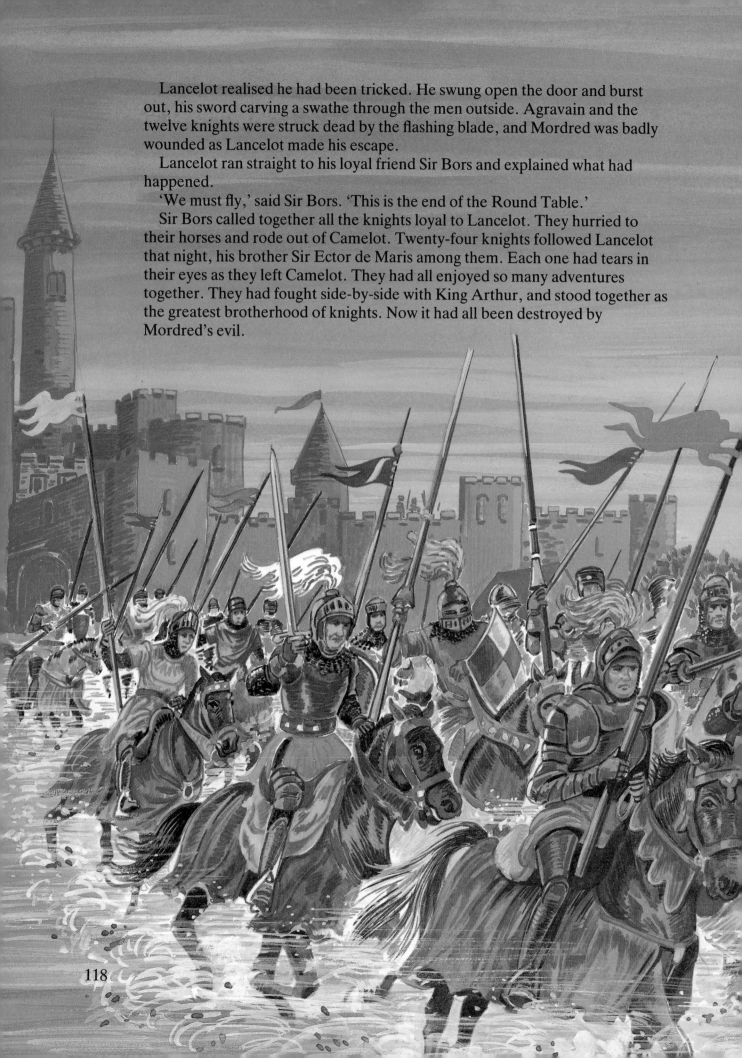

Lancelot realised he had been tricked. He swung open the door and burst out, his sword carving a swathe through the men outside. Agravain and the twelve knights were struck dead by the flashing blade, and Mordred was badly wounded as Lancelot made his escape.

Lancelot ran straight to his loyal friend Sir Bors and explained what had happened.

'We must fly,' said Sir Bors. 'This is the end of the Round Table.'

Sir Bors called together all the knights loyal to Lancelot. They hurried to their horses and rode out of Camelot. Twenty-four knights followed Lancelot that night, his brother Sir Ector de Maris among them. Each one had tears in their eyes as they left Camelot. They had all enjoyed so many adventures together. They had fought side-by-side with King Arthur, and stood together as the greatest brotherhood of knights. Now it had all been destroyed by Mordred's evil.

Meanwhile, in the castle, Mordred ran to King Arthur with the news that Lancelot had escaped from Guinevere's chamber and had killed Agravain.

'Look, my Lord,' said Mordred, 'these wounds I bear were made by Lancelot. Surely you see him now for the traitor he is. The queen herself cannot be excused. She must die.'

The king's face turned white and tears welled up in his eyes. 'I would give my life not to have Sir Lancelot against me. But what's happened tonight has destroyed the fellowship of the Round Table.'

In the days that followed, Lancelot gathered new supporters wherever he went. Soon he had hundreds of knights ready to fight for him. But with every mile he travelled, Lancelot grew more worried about Guinevere. Would the king put her to death?

At Camelot, the king was holding a council with the knights who remained with him. Mordred spoke first, demanding both the death of the queen and war against Lancelot. But Gawain was not convinced.

'My Lord, Lancelot is the noblest knight who ever lived. Think again. We all know Mordred and Agravain are just troublemakers.'

But the king knew he was in an impossible position. 'This is the last thing I wanted in the world,' he said, 'but Mordred has the law on his side. The queen must die. I can take no other course.'

The king fell silent for a moment and then turned to Gawain. 'The queen will go nobly to her death,' he said, 'but I would like you and your brothers Gaheris and Gareth to escort her to the fire. You are her friends and it will give her some comfort.'

119

Gawain was horrified. 'I cannot. I could not bear to see such a noble lady meet such a shameful and undeserved death.'

'Then,' said the king, 'Gaheris and Gareth must be there.'

Gaheris and Gareth reluctantly agreed on the understanding that they would not wear armour or carry weapons. 'It would be disrespectful to the queen to wear the clothes of war on such a sad day,' said Gaheris.

The queen's execution was planned for two days later. The court of Camelot was in mourning when the day dawned. The king saw Guinevere before she left and begged her to forgive him for what was to happen.

'I forgive you with all my heart,' she said. 'You have been misled by traitors. The fire may take my life, but my soul will honour you forever.'

The king was heartbroken as Gaheris and Gareth led her out of the castle and to the field of execution. Guinevere said her last prayers and then Gareth and Gaheris led her toward the stake. The executioner lit his torch.

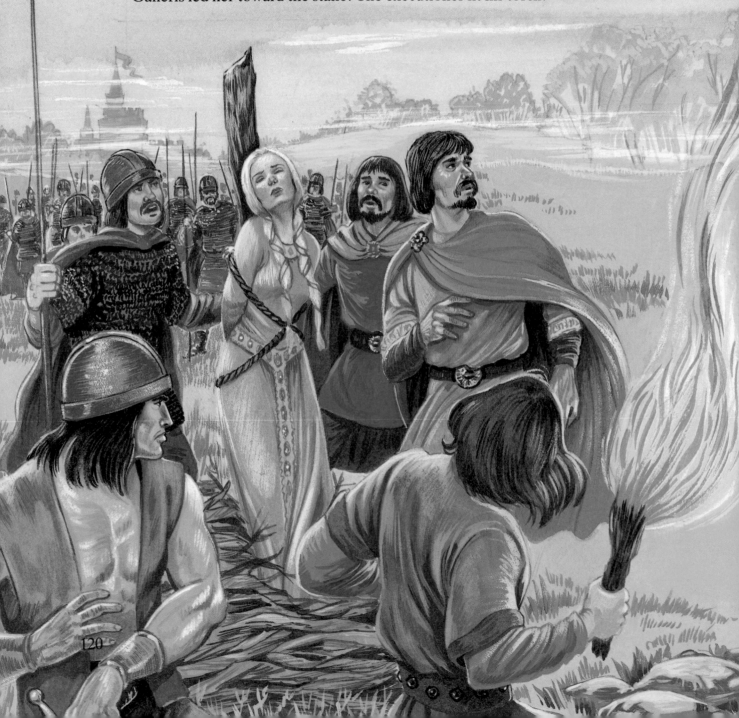

'Put out your torch, executioner!' boomed a voice on the edge of the field.

Guinevere recognised the voice immediately. Sir Lancelot galloped out of the wood towards the fire. Never had Lancelot ridden with such power and speed, his sword flashing in the morning sunlight. His blade sliced through the air in all directions, but his eye was fixed on Guinevere. As he reached her, he was vaguely conscious of his sword striking something. But he didn't have time to look at what it was. His only aim was to make sure he rescued Guinevere. He leaned down at the last moment and, catching her around the waist, drew her onto his horse.

The crowd watched in disbelief as Lancelot and Guinevere disappeared into the forest.

The silence was broken by Mordred who cried out when he saw two bodies by the fire. Gaheris and Gareth lay dead. In the wild gallop past the fire, Lancelot's sword had accidentally caught the two brothers. They had not been wearing armour and Lancelot's sword had cut two mortal blows.

Lancelot did not stop until he reached the camp where all his supporters had gathered. Sir Bors was worried when he heard what had happened. 'This can only mean war,' he said. 'The king will come to claim his queen.'

'The king will have his queen,' said Lancelot. 'But she will stay with us until the king comes to his senses and realises who the real traitors are. Come, we ride north.'

Lancelot and his army broke camp. Within a few days they had reached his northern fortress, the Castle of Joy. And there they waited for King Arthur.

The Siege at Lancelot's Castle

'Who killed them? Tell me who killed them?' Gawain had just heard that his brothers Gaheris and Gareth were dead.

King Arthur whispered his answer. 'Sir Lancelot.'

'No!' cried Gawain. 'He could never have done such a terrible deed. My brothers were not even wearing armour.'

The king said nobody could tell how it happened, but it was Lancelot's sword which had taken their lives.

Gawain roared out angrily, 'These deaths will be avenged. I will never rest until I have killed Lancelot. Even if I have to ride through seven kingdoms, I will seek him out. King Arthur, we must prepare for war!'

The king knew that war was inevitable and gave orders for preparations to begin. That night he sat alone at the Round Table. He looked at all the seats and thought of all the knights who had sat there over the years.

'Oh that things should have come to this,' he cried. 'Yet, Merlin said it would happen. He foretold that one of my own family would bring me great troubles. Mordred is more to blame for this than anyone else.'

Arthur took out his sword Excalibur and ran his fingers affectionately along the blade. 'You have served me well,' he said, 'yet I will not carry you with me in the battle to come. You were never meant to kill people who were once my friends.'

Then Arthur let out a great cry of anguish. 'I would give my kingdom to see the return of all my Knights of the Round Table, to hear their stories and adventures; to see them go out to do battle for me. It's all gone. The days of the Round Table are over.'

The next day, knights who were still loyal to King Arthur gathered at Camelot. The courtyard was filled with men, horses and armour. Arthur gave them their orders. 'We march on Lancelot. We must bring Guinevere back.'

Gawain interrupted. 'And Lancelot's head!'

King Arthur's army marched north. Many more warriors joined him on the way. It was a huge army which finally reached the Castle of Joy. That night, under a full moon, they camped beneath the castle battlements.

The king lay in his tent, his mind much troubled by what was to come. Then he heard Lancelot's voice call out from the battlements above.

'Arthur, King of all the Britons, I shall not fight you. My honour would not let me hurt the dearest king that ever was.'

'Fie on you Lancelot,' answered the king, looking up to the castle walls. He could see Lancelot silhouetted by the moon. 'You have killed Gawain's young brothers.'

'Their deaths happened by chance,' said Lancelot. 'I loved them as dearly as anyone. It happened in the heat of the moment and I surely never meant to kill them.'

'And you stole away with the queen,' said Arthur.

'I only came to rescue my queen from a shameful death, one she didn't deserve. She has done no wrong. Nor I. I will only keep her here until you realise that you been deceived by evil men such as Mordred and Agravain. The queen belongs to you and always will.'

Gawain stepped forward. 'Silence traitor! The king will have both his queen and your head. Only your life can make up for the death of my dear brothers.'

Lancelot repeated that he had never intended to kill Gaheris and Gareth, but Gawain's blood was up.

'You lie, traitor,' he cried, 'and if there is any nobility left in you, come out and face us on the battlefield.'

Lancelot's knights were furious at Gawain's insults, and demanded to be allowed to fight.

'Gawain will not be silenced with words,' said Sir Bors. 'We must take to the battlefield.'

'That is the sad truth,' said Lancelot. 'But when we battle every one of my knights must make sure that neither King Arthur nor Gawain are killed.'

The next morning King Arthur's men were ready as Lancelot led his own army into the field. A moment later a thousand knights clashed together in bloody battle. Lancelot fought in the thick of things with Sir Bors at his side. Arthur and Gawain saw them and attacked. King Arthur was knocked from his horse in the fight, and Lancelot could have killed him where he lay. But he didn't. Instead, Lancelot dismounted and helped Arthur onto his horse again.

'My Lord,' he said. 'Stop this battle now. We have nothing to fight about.'

Arthur looked into Lancelot's eyes and saw once again the noble knight of old.

'Alas,' cried the king, 'that this war should ever have begun.'

But the battle raged on until sunset when both armies retired to bury their dead. The next morning the combat began again. And so it went on for many days. Hundreds of knights from both sides died in the slaughter. But Lancelot's men kept their promise. The king and Gawain were not harmed.

Lancelot could bear it no longer. He hated the sight of knights, who had once been his comrades, dying. 'Something must be done,' he said, 'or else there will be no one left alive on this evil battlefield.'

The next morning, as King Arthur stood ready for battle again, the castle gates opened. An extraordinary sight met his eyes. A hundred knights, all dressed in green, rode out with Lancelot at their head. Not one was armed. Instead, each man carried an olive branch as a token of peace. Suddenly a flash of white caught Arthur's eye. In the middle of the men he saw Guinevere being carried on a bier.

Lancelot stopped in front of Arthur. 'My Lord, I bring you your queen as I promised. I will fight no more. I would rather banish myself from this land than see more blood spilt.'

King Arthur was ready to forgive his favourite knight, but Gawain was still determined to have his revenge. 'You had no excuse for killing my brothers. You can go to the end of the world and I will find you.'

'I will tell you where you can find me,' said Lancelot. 'This day I leave for France. If you come after me I shall be in my father's castle at Benwick.'

It was late afternoon when Lancelot and his men left the Castle of Joy and took the road for the coast. Lancelot looked back as the sun set behind his castle. 'I will not return here again,' he cried. 'In future this place will be known as the Castle of Misery.'

123

Mordred's Treachery

Lancelot and his men reached the coast and sailed for France, safely reaching his father's lands at Benwick. Lancelot immediately ordered his knights and the townsfolk to prepare for a siege. He knew the avenging Gawain would not be far behind him.

King Arthur only wanted peace with Lancelot, but he felt honour bound to do what Gawain wanted. And Gawain would never rest until either he or Lancelot were dead.

Arthur realised that if he went to France he would have to appoint someone to look after his kingdom while he was away. There was only one person he could choose because he was of royal blood. But he was the man Arthur mistrusted most; his nephew Mordred.

The scheming Mordred saw his chance. He went to Arthur and swore he had not meant to cause all the trouble which had happened between the king and Lancelot.

'Give me the chance to make amends,' he begged. 'I will look after your kingdom.'

If Arthur ever had a weakness, it was to trust people too much. He left his kingdom in the hands of Mordred and sailed for France with Gawain and an army of sixty thousand men. The army was so strong that no one stood in Arthur's way when he landed. He soon reached the town of Benwick.

Once again Lancelot would not send out his knights to fight for fear of killing the king and his old comrades. Gawain rode up to the castle walls and shouted to Lancelot, 'Come out and fight, traitor!'

128

Lancelot knew that Gawain would never be satisfied without a fight. 'Noble Gawain,' he called, 'this fight is not between me and King Arthur. This is our battle and so I will fight you. But let no other man be involved.'

Lancelot saddled his strongest horse and put on his full armour. Then he rode out to meet Gawain.

'I agree to your terms,' said Gawain. 'No man will come between us.'

King Arthur's sixty thousand men stood back to watch, as did thousands of others on the battlements of Benwick.

'This is a battle to the death,' cried Gawain. 'One of us will not leave this field alive.'

The two great knights, their lances raised, spurred their horses into a charge. No man had ever seen knights ride with such fury and passion. The two challengers were almost hidden by the clouds of dust raised by the racing hooves. And in those clouds, they met like thunder and lightning, lances rattling each other's shield. The horses' nostrils flared as they charged again. When they met this time, both men's lances broke in half. But still they charged again, hacking at each with their broken weapons. Both men's shields shattered into pieces.

Swords were drawn as they rode at each other once more, Gawain fiercely lashing out at Lancelot, who parried the blow. And so it went on all morning, with Gawain attacking and Lancelot defending every blow. By midday the horses were so tired that they both collapsed with exhaustion beneath their riders. The battle continued on foot.

Gawain seemed like a man possessed as he ran in with his blade swirling in the air. Every now and then Gawain struck home, and soon Lancelot's body was cut in many places. But, as the afternoon wore on, Gawain tired a little and Lancelot took his chance. His blade found its mark on Gawain's helmet. It split and the sword pierced his skull. He fell to the ground.

'Finish it, Lancelot,' said Gawain. 'I will not ask for mercy.'

But Lancelot walked away and went back into the castle. 'I will never kill a man who was once my friend,' he shouted.

'I'll be back,' said Gawain, as he was carried from the battlefield.

It took Gawain three weeks to recover from his wound, and, as soon as he was fit, he rode out again.

The fight was as fierce as the first and ended with the same result. They fought all day until Lancelot struck again. Once more Gawain was carried from the field, swearing to return.

Gawain was healed within the month and ready to challenge Lancelot again. But on the morning that he was due to ride out, a messenger galloped into King Arthur's camp.

'My Lord, grave news,' he gasped, almost out of breath from his ride, 'Mordred has told the people that you have been killed in France. And now he has been crowned King of England. There's even talk he wants to marry Queen Guinevere!'

'I should never have trusted my wicked nephew,' roared King Arthur. 'I will have his life for it.'

King Arthur ordered an immediate return to England. Lancelot watched in amazement as Arthur, Gawain and their sixty thousand knights broke camp and marched away.

Mordred was waiting for King Arthur at Dover. There was a ferocious battle on the beaches. But Arthur's men put Mordred and his men to flight.

Arthur counted his casualties and found they were slight, but then his butlers Sir Bedevere and Sir Lucan came rushing over.

'Gawain is badly hurt, my Lord,' they cried.

Arthur found Gawain lying in one of the boats. Blood was trickling from a deep wound in his head.

'It is a mortal wound,' sighed Gawain. 'I will not last out the day. I beg you bring me quill and paper. I have a final letter to write.'

Materials were brought and Gawain weakly raised himself up on his elbow so he could write.

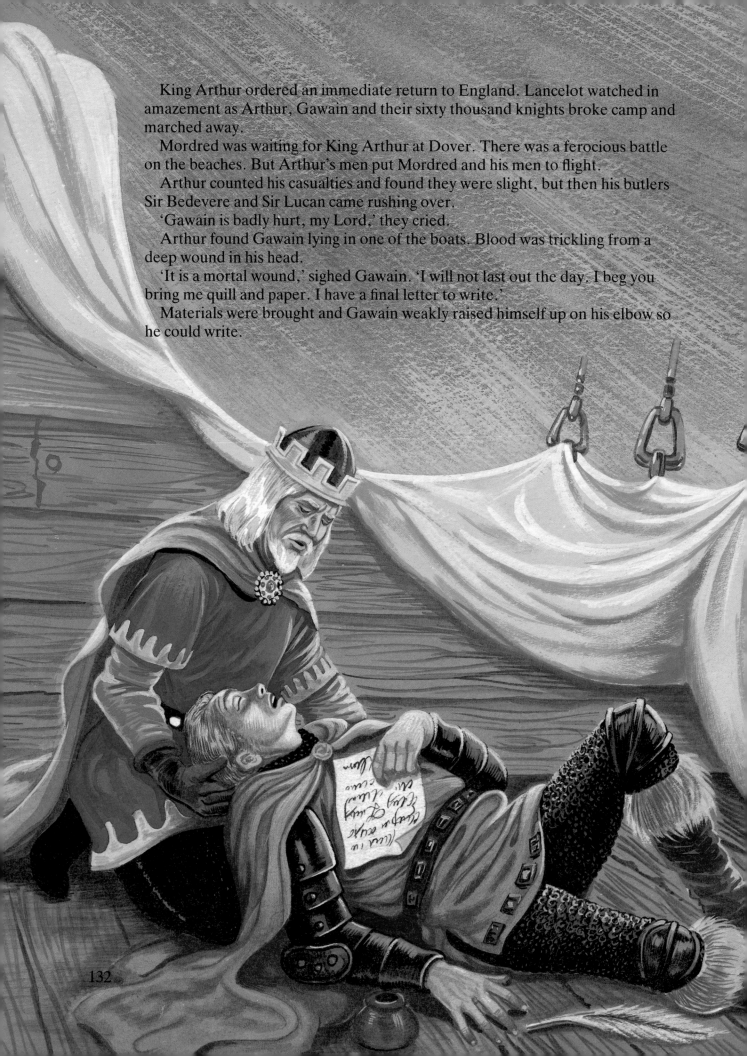

132

"To my Noble Sir Lancelot,
I lie wounded to death on England's dear shore. As my end approaches I must beg your forgiveness. It was for the love of my brothers that I swore revenge on you. Yet, in death, my head has cleared. I know that you would never have slain them on purpose. I know that you loved Gaheris and Gareth as much as I. Indeed, I know it was a noble deed you did that day in rescuing Queen Guinevere. King Arthur knows it too. And he needs your help once more. This day we drove this scoundrel Mordred inland, but even now he is gathering a great army to destroy our rightful king. I beg you to do one more gallant deed in the name of the Round Table. Hurry back to England with your men to save the kingdom …"

Gawain signed his name and then added a note at the bottom.
"… One more request I make. Visit my tomb when you reach England."
They were the last words that Gawain wrote. He slumped back and died. King Arthur cradled Gawain's head in his lap and wept. That night, even as Gawain was buried in Dover Castle, the letter was on its way by messenger to France.

The Death of King Arthur

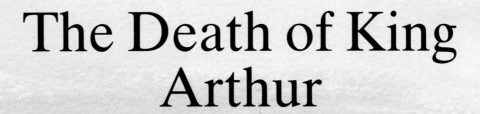

The moon was rising over Dover Castle as Gawain's ghost slipped into King Arthur's dreams. 'Be warned,' he said, 'don't fight with Mordred yet. Call a truce to give Lancelot time to reach you with help.'

In the morning King Arthur sent messengers to Mordred asking for a peace council. Mordred agreed and the next day both armies faced each other on the downs north of Dover.

King Arthur, fearing Mordred's treachery, warned his own men to be ready to attack if they saw anything suspicious. Then he sat down to talk with his untrustworthy nephew.

At that moment an adder crawled from the undergrowth and bit one of Mordred's knights. The knight drew his sword and cut off the snake's head. But Arthur's men saw the blade flashing in the sunlight. Suspecting Mordred was double-crossing their king, the trumpets were sounded and Arthur's army charged into battle.

King Arthur had no choice but to ride back and join his men. The two great armies thundered down towards each other and met with a bloody clash of arms. It was Arthur's last great battle and thousands of knights had died by the time a blood-red sunset filled the sky at the end of that summer day.

The fighting went on until both armies had been destroyed. Arthur wept as he saw how many good knights he had lost. An army of ghosts left the battlefield as the evening mists crept in.

Arthur saw that only two Knights of the Round Table had survived the battle, his loyal servants Sir Bedevere and Sir Lucan, who, himself, was so badly wounded he would not live long.

Arthur suddenly remembered his sword Excalibur. He had not carried it with him since he had left Camelot to lay siege to Lancelot's castle. He asked Sir Bedevere to ride to Camelot to fetch it. 'I will have need of Excalibur today,' said Arthur.

135

Sir Bedevere rode off and Arthur went out to search the battlefield for any signs of life. Death was all around him. But suddenly the mists cleared and he saw a figure walking towards him. It was Mordred!

Arthur heard Merlin's prophesy ringing in his head. 'Treachery from one of your own family will bring your death on the battlefield. Beware the traitor!'

But Arthur's fury at seeing Mordred blinded him to the warning he had been given so many years before. He raised his lance and charged. 'Die, traitor!' he cried.

The lance speared Mordred through his chest. But, as the power of the thrust hurled him into the air, Mordred grasped his own sword with both hands and brought it down on Arthur's head.

When Arthur recovered consciousness, Sir Bedevere had returned with Excalibur. Not far away lay the dead body of Mordred, and, close by, that of Sir Lucan who had breathed his last rushing to the king's help.

'I have killed Mordred,' said Arthur. 'Yet he has dealt me a mortal blow, too. Sir Bedevere I have one last task for you.'

136

Arthur told Bedevere to take the sword to the lake from where Excalibur had come. 'Long ago I promised Nimue, the Lady of the Lake that I would return Excalibur,' said the king. 'Take it now, and throw it into the depths.'

Bedevere rode off again with the sword. When he reached the lake, he could not bring himself to throw away such a valuable weapon. He hid it instead and returned to Arthur.

'What did you see?' asked Arthur, his life ebbing away.

'Nothing, my Lord,' said Bedevere. 'Just a splash.'

'You lie,' said the king. 'Return to the lake and do as I asked you.'

Bedevere rode back to the lake, but still he couldn't throw it in. He hid it again. When he returned, Arthur asked him the same question and once more Bedevere lied.

'Bedevere,' cried Arthur. 'I'll give you one last chance. Return to the lake and do as I say. Throw the sword into the depths.'

Bedevere had no idea how the king knew he was lying. But this time he did throw the sword into the lake.

Bedevere returned to Arthur with the answer the king had waited for.

'I threw the sword into the lake,' said Bedevere, 'and such a strange thing happened. A hand appeared and grasped the sword. Three times the sword circled in the air and then the hand took it beneath the surface. It vanished.'

'T"is nothing strange,' said Arthur. 'The good sword Excalibur has returned to where it came from. Now carry me to the lake.'

Sir Bedevere put King Arthur on his horse and led him away from the battlefield. The last light of day was fading when they reached the lake. Chilly mists rolled eerily across the water.

Bedevere laid Arthur on a bank of moss by the lake's edge. The king had lost so much blood from Mordred's wound that his face had turned a ghostly white.

'Someone is coming, my Lord,' said Bedevere, hearing a gentle ripple out on the lake.

A barge drifted out of the mists. Bedevere stepped back in fright. Nimue, the Lady of the Lake, was standing on the prow beckoning to King Arthur.

'Put me aboard, Sir Bedevere,' said Arthur. 'Nimue has come to take me on my last journey.'

Bedevere carried Arthur aboard and laid him with his head resting gently in Nimue's lap.

'You were faithful to your promise, King Arthur,' she said. 'You returned the sword Excalibur. Someone else may have need of it one day.'

The barge drifted away from the side of the lake and slowly vanished in the mists.

Sir Bedevere called out, 'My Lord, tell me where you are going. Will we see you again?'

A ghostly voice echoed from the gloom. 'Death takes me now. My journey's end is the Vale of Avalon. There will I find the spirits of my dear companions who once sat at the Round Table.'

Darkness fell and an owl swooped silently across the lake. Arthur, King of all the Britons, was dead.

Story's End

So the story of King Arthur ends. Lancelot reached England and found he was too late to help his king. But he kept his promise to Gawain. He visited his old comrade's grave at Dover Castle.

Lancelot saw Guinevere just once more. He visited her at the nunnery where she had gone after hearing of the king's death. It was Guinevere who persuaded Lancelot to begin a new life. He became a monk and spent the rest of his days in a monastery.

When Lancelot died, a hundred knights carrying a hundred candles, escorted his body back to the Castle of Joy. There, the boldest Knight of the Round Table was buried.

The story is told that King Arthur, after his journey to the spirit kingdom of Avalon, was buried at the dead of night near Glastonbury. When Guinevere died, she was buried beside him.